Girl on the Other Side

Deborah Kerbel

Girl on the Other Side

a novel

DUNDURN PRESS
TORONTO

Edited by Shannon Whibbs
Designed by Courtney Horner
Printed and bound in Canada by Webcom

Library and Archives Canada Cataloguing in Publication

Kerbel, Deborah
      Girl on the other side / by Deborah Kerbel.

ISBN 978-1-55488-443-8

      I. Title.

PS8621.E75G57 2009   jC813'.6   C2009-903258-9

1 2 3 4 5   13 12 11 10 09

Canadä

**Conseil des Arts
du Canada**   **Canada Council
for the Arts**

**ONTARIO ARTS COUNCIL
CONSEIL DES ARTS DE L'ONTARIO**

We acknowledge the support of the **Canada Council for the Arts** and the **Ontario Arts Council** for our publishing program. We also acknowledge the financial support of the **Government of Canada** through the **Book Publishing Industry Development Program** and **The Association for the Export of Canadian Books**, and the **Government of Ontario** through the **Ontario Book Publishers Tax Credit program**, and the **Ontario Media Development Corporation**.

Care has been taken to trace the ownership of copyright material used in this book. The author and the publisher welcome any information enabling them to rectify any references or credits in subsequent editions.

J. Kirk Howard, President

Printed and Bound in Canada.
www.dundurn.com

Dundurn Press	Gazelle Book Services Limited	Dundurn Press
3 Church Street, Suite 500	White Cross Mills	2250 Military Road
Toronto, Ontario, Canada	High Town, Lancaster, England	Tonawanda, NY
M5E 1M2	LA1 4XS	U.S.A. 14150

© **Mixed Sources**
Product group from well-managed
forests, controlled sources and
recycled wood or fiber
FSC www.fsc.org Cert no. SW-COC-002358
© 1996 Forest Stewardship Council

97%

ANCIENT FOREST ™
FRIENDLY

For my Mom

Who fought back hard and never lost her smile

tabby

The toilet flushes beside me. A loud, liquid sucking sound rises up from the stall and echoes off the green tiled walls of the girls' bathroom. I peek under the door and watch as a beat-up pair of sandals trudges across the floor toward the sink. Then suddenly they're gone.

Without even washing her hands! Ew!

I'm alone again. I breathe a deep sigh of relief, trying not to take any air in through my nose. The smells in this place are nauseating — a mix of cheap soap, bleach, and pee. I feel like I might be sick. Shifting my weight on the hard plastic seat, I check my watch for the hundredth time. Still twenty minutes left of lunch period. My butt is getting numb from sitting for so long. But I can't go back out there. Not after what they've been saying about me.

The door creaks open. A moment later, a different pair of shoes appear in the stall beside me. These ones are cleaner, newer, trendier.

These ones will wash their hands, I think to myself.

The sound of a zipper, a shuffling of clothes, followed by ...

I cover my ears so I won't have to find out and swallow the sharp acid taste that's suddenly on my tongue. *Gross!* I think I just threw up a bit in my mouth.

The girls' bathroom is a disgusting place to hang out. But trust me, you'd do the same if you were in my shoes. Which, by the way, are pretty fantastic.

Kind of like how I *used* to be.

Suddenly, a pair of dirty sneakers flies across the green tiles and lands in the stall directly to my left. The door crashes shut and the sound of sobbing fills my ears. I lean down and examine the shoes beside me for clues as the crying quickly rises into an ear-splitting moan.

Lora

Thank God ... school hasn't been so bad lately. Not since they found someone new to pick on. Still, I'm careful to keep under the radar. At lunchtime, I choose an empty table in a quiet corner of the cafeteria and eat quickly, hoping to avoid trouble. But halfway through my sandwich it starts.

"Hey, Frog-face!"

I freeze mid-chew. *Please leave me alone*, I think, sitting perfectly still. You might not know this, but bullies are like dogs — they'll chase you harder if you run.

"Did you hear me?"

Gulping the lump of cheese and bread down, I hold my breath and pretend I don't hear … pretend it doesn't hurt. But of course, it does. You'd think I'd be used to the teasing by now — it's been happening ever since first grade. My eyes dart around the perimeter of the cafeteria, searching for a teacher. But there's nobody in sight.

"Hey, show some manners — we're talking to you!" another voice calls.

I begin to quietly wrap the rest of my sandwich up, all the while imagining myself inside an invisible bubble — a magic force field where their words can't penetrate.

But out of my peripheral vision I see a group of tough-looking boys walking toward my table. Their smiles send chills up my spine. I don't know these boys personally, but I know their type all too well. Rough, rude, and vicious — like pit bulls, the meanest dogs of all. I ball up the remains of my lunch and jump to my feet. Instinct has taken over my body — dogs or no dogs, it's time to start running! But the boys are too fast. They grab me by the shoulders and push me back down onto the hard wooden bench.

"Jake just wants to see if he's a prince," they laugh, as they push me down farther. Down, down, until the back of my head smacks against the crummy, sticky cafeteria floor with a painful *thud*. Tiny pinpricks of light float in front of my eyes.

"Stop! Let go!" I gasp. But they don't listen. They don't even hear me. Two of them hold my arms while the third one sits on my stomach. My half-eaten sandwich rises up in my throat. If only I could projectile-vomit on command.

"Do it! Do it!" the two at my arms shout at the third. Terrified, I watch as the guy they call Jake closes his eyes, leans forward and smashes his lips down onto mine. His eyes are squeezed so tightly shut it looks like he's in pain — like he's the one being attacked instead of me. A second later it's over. Releasing my arms, they stand up and walk away, leaving me lying there on the dirty floor like a piece of trash.

"Damn, that's the last time I lose a bet to you guys," the pit bull named Jake says, wiping his mouth on his sleeve. His friends laugh and punch each other in the arms.

The world around me blurs as I pull myself to my feet and dash out of the cafeteria. Dozens of laughing faces whiz by me as I run.

"Croak ... croak ... croak ..." sing the chorus of teen-fiends at my back.

I stagger to the girls' bathroom and lock myself in the last stall. Burying my face in my hands, I begin to sob so hard I can barely catch my breath. My life's mantra escapes from my mouth in a low, soggy moan:

I hate them ... I hate them ... I hate them ... I hate them ...

After a couple of minutes, I grab some toilet paper and mop up my face. Trying to calm myself down in time for my next class, I inhale deeply and imagine myself far away from this place. It's the only thing that gives me any comfort — the idea that one day soon, this will all be over.

A light tapping at the right side of the stall interrupts my thoughts.

"Um ... hello? You okay in there?" whispers a voice.

Okay, wait. I think we need to rewind a couple of months ...

tabby

They hang on my every word ... follow me around like a pack of eager puppies ... treat me like some sort of rock star. Right now they're watching me eat. I take a bite of my yogurt. Their eyes follow the spoon as it travels to my mouth. Wait and see, tomorrow they'll all bring low-fat raspberry yogurt for lunch. Just like me.

It's always been this way. When you belong to the richest family in town, people treat you like you're something special. Sometimes, I believe it, too. But other times I want to yell at them. Call them idiots. Nanny Beth would call them sheep — that's probably a better word.

Leave me alone! I feel like shouting. But instead I just smile and look cool — as usual. I take another bite of my yogurt, enjoying the smooth sweetness in my mouth for a few extra seconds before swallowing, then push the half-eaten container away and reach for my carrot sticks.

"Aren't you going to finish that?" asks Brandi, eyeing the yogurt. Annoyed, I nibble on my carrot and ignore her. For God's sake, she's known me long enough to know the answer to that question. No matter what I'm eating or how

hungry I am, I always leave part of my meal untouched —
it's one of the "food rules" Catherine insists on. Another
one of her rules is that our cupboards are only filled with
healthy, low-fat, low-carb choices. Catherine's put Nanny
under strict orders not to let me eat any junk food. Because,
God forbid her daughter be anything but model-thin. It
sounds harsh, but I've been eating this way for so long now,
I don't know how to stop — even when I'm at school and
Catherine's nowhere nearby.

By the way, in case you're wondering, Catherine is my
mother. I've been using her first name for years.

"The word 'Mommy' makes me feel so old and stuffy,
darling," she'd said. It was the night of my sixth birthday
when she was tucking me into bed. A rare event.

"And anyway, I'm more of a friend than a parent, right?"

I remember the way her eyes stole over to her reflection
in my mirrored closet doors while she waited for my reply.
I'd said "yes" quickly, because I knew that's what she wanted
me to do. After she'd left my room, I cried a bit at losing my
"Mommy," but not as much as you'd think. She was never
much of one anyway.

Brandi must know I'm mad because she starts lobbing
compliments at me.

"Great sweater, Tab, where'd you get it? Hey, do you
need a lift home today? My mom can take you ..."

I hear the desperation rising in her voice. She wants
me to let her know everything's okay. Just one little word
of approval is all she needs from me. For a moment, I

consider giving it to her. After all, I know just how powerful words can be.

When I was three, I learned how to say the f-word. Nanny told me what I was actually trying to say was "fire truck" but my tongue got tangled around the sounds. Even though I didn't know what it meant, every time I said it, a grown-up would freak out. It was incredible. I remember being amazed that one little word could make people so upset. Think about it — just one letter away from kid-approved words like "duck" and "tuck," but it drove people crazy — my parents especially. Which, naturally, just made me say it even more. Back then, I lived for their attention.

In the end, I decide to make Brandi squirm.

"So Dylan, what are you doing after school?" I ask my other BFF — who happens to be Brandi's twin sister. Out of the corner of my eye, I see Brandi's face. She looks constipated, like she's using every muscle in her head to hold back those tears.

I feel a tap on my shoulder and glance up. Derek Blair is looking down at me with his creamy caramel brown eyes and his trademark too-cool-for-school lip-curling half-smile. My heart bounces inside my chest.

"Hey," he says, raising his perfectly shaped eyebrows. I wonder if they grow that way naturally or if he has them waxed. Or plucked?

"Hey," I reply, dropping just the right amount of chill into my voice to shoot his hopes down. Then I turn away and continue talking to Dylan. I know Derek likes me. He's been dropping lots of not-so-subtle hints over the past few weeks ... like leaving me messages and wall posts on Facebook and acting funny and immature around me so I'll notice him. I definitely like him, too, but I have to pretend I don't. It's a well known fact that guys enjoy a good chase. My plan is to wait until the end of the term to let him catch me. He is, after all, the hottest guy in the entire school. It's like destiny that we get together.

When lunch is over, I wave goodbye to my friends and head for my locker. I pass Frog-face on the way down the main hall. As usual, there's a small group of kids following her and calling out names. Like everyone else in my grade, I've known Lora Froggett since kindergarten — she's always been an easy target. I bet you know someone like that too — the kind of kid who won't stand up for herself. If it were me getting picked on like that, I'd fight back. But Frog-face never does. If you ask me, she practically begs to be teased. I don't know why, though. If she cleaned herself up, washed her hair more often, stood up straight, and wore better shoes, she probably wouldn't be half bad. But with a name like Froggett, she's probably been doomed from the start. It's a classic example of "the chicken and the egg" — did her last name turn her into a victim, or was she born that way to begin with?

I pause in front of my open locker and watch the group chase her. Trying her best to ignore them, she hurries down the hall, her arms filled with books and her shoulders hunched against their insults. One girl suddenly runs ahead, sticks her foot out and trips Frog-face. Books go flying. The hall rings with laughter. I'm the only one who doesn't join in. Well, except Frog-face, of course. My stomach feels sick as I watch her go down. I hate watching people fall. It reminds me of my nightmare — I've been having the same one for years.

In it, I'm always on the roof of a tall building, standing at the edge, looking down. Even though I want to move away to safety, I never can. Night after night I just stand there, teetering and wobbling and swinging my arms wildly, trying to keep my balance and not drop over the edge. But somehow, I always end up falling. The way down is a long, terrifying nosedive through the clouds. As I rush toward the ground, I scream and flap my arms like a baby bird trying to fly. It's out of control and totally terrifying. I always wake up just before I crash, always in a panicky, full-body sweat. Thankfully I have Sam. He sleeps at the end of my bed and I'm convinced it's because of him that I never hit the ground. He always seems to know when the dream is happening and nudges me awake with his nose in the nick of time.

Sam dreams, too. Maybe that's one of the reasons why he understands me so well. I know he dreams because I've watched him panting and barking this strange, muffled noise while he sleeps. Beagles are hound dogs — Nanny says it's in his genes to chase rabbits. I don't think he's actually ever seen a rabbit in real life. But I'm positive that's what he's chasing in his dreams.

The first bell rings, crashing through my thoughts like an alarm. I turn away from the sight of Frog-face picking up her spilled books. Closing my locker, I stroll into my English class and slide into my seat. Miss Wall is writing something on the whiteboard. Her wide butt wiggles grotesquely with every stroke of the marker. Miss Wall is a total mess. Her hair is unbrushed, the tags of her clothes stick out, her pants are so tight that everyone can see the doughy rolls of fat underneath the thin, polyester fabric, and her shirts (which never match) are covered in coffee stains. And her shoes — ugh! She always wears the same pair of beat-up Birkenstocks, no matter what the season. In the summer, her yellow, cracked nails go bare for the world to see. And in the winter, she layers those ratty sandals with wool socks — the ultimate fashion "don't." On top of all that, she's always picking gooey gunk out of her eyes and ears. Thank God she leaves her nose alone. Otherwise, I swear, I'd have to walk out.

Miss Wall is mesmerizing in her messiness. Like a car wreck you just can't take your eyes off of. But she irritates me, too. Sometimes, I want to shake her by the shoulders and slap some neatness into her.

If Lora Froggett doesn't watch out, that's what she'll turn into one day. Old, fat, unmarried, and the butt of everyone's jokes.

Lora

"Get up, Frog-face!" hisses a voice from above.

I'm sprawled on the floor of the main hallway, my books scattered in every direction.

Frog-face. That's me.

At least, that's what kids at school call me. I hear it so much, I'm surprised when they use my real name.

Sticks and stones may break my bones, but names will never hurt me.

Whoever came up with that saying wasn't too bright. I broke my leg in two places in the first grade. I was running away from a bully who was calling me names, fell down the school steps and ended up in traction for a month. Sure my leg hurt, but that was nothing compared to the verbal bashing I've taken over the years. I've been called every name you can imagine: Toad-girl, Frog-legs, Polliwog, Croaker, Swamp-thing, Tadpole, Warty, Pond-scum, and of course, Frog-face. For some reason, that's the one that's stuck.

The first bell rings, signalling the end of lunch. Sneakers stomp all around me as kids rush to their classes. Naturally, nobody stops to help me as I scramble to pick up my books in the midst of the stampede. In fact, it's all I can do to keep my fingers from being crushed as I reach to save my books from getting trampled. One by one, I gather them back in my arms and hold them close to my chest. These books are the most precious things I own ... my tickets out of this place.

"Crawl back to your swamp!" some girl sneers as I pull myself up off the floor.

I ignore the comment and the piranha who made it and hurry down the hall to my English class. I call the popular mean girls in my school "piranhas" because they almost always attack in packs and they can chew you to pieces before you know what hit you.

This year is turning out to be worse than ever. Maybe it's because the piranhas are beginning to date the pit bulls. I remember reading that animals display their physical prowess to the opposite sex by attacking other, less dominant, animals. If that's true, it would explain a lot of stuff going on at my school this year.

Tabby Freeman walks in to class just ahead of me. She's the head piranha — the one all the other girls look up to and copy. She isn't the prettiest girl in school, but her family is the richest and most powerful in town and that matters a lot more than looks around here.

I plop into my seat just as the second bell rings. Putting down her marker, Miss Wall turns around to face us. She catches my eye and her face crinkles into a wide smile. I smile back. Miss Wall is my favourite teacher this year. Maybe my favourite teacher ever. Plump and pleasant and gray-haired, she reminds me of a grandmother — not my own, of course. I never actually had a grandparent — all four of them died before I was born. Clearly our family's DNA has serious flaws. But I guess that's pretty obvious when you look at my mother. She was diagnosed with primary-progressive Multiple Sclerosis a few months after my baby brother Cody was born. Although at first the symptoms were mild, they got bad really fast. Mommy's a different person now than she was four years ago — unsteady on her feet and exhausted and weak all the time. Sometimes weeks go by when she doesn't get out of bed except to use the bathroom. Daddy tries to help, but he isn't around very much. He's a firefighter and works crazy shifts so when he's home he ends up sleeping a lot, because his body clock is so turned around. Most of the time, I'm on my own taking care of the house, my baby brother and two little sisters, and the pets, of course. I try not to complain. Compared to what Mommy's dealing with, my problems are pretty insignificant.

"Today we're about to embark on an adventure," Miss Wall says, picking up a thin paperback book from her desk. "And I promise it will be an adventure you'll never forget."

She holds up the book. It's *Romeo and Juliet*. The class groans in unison. I'm not surprised. This is probably the first time any of them had ever been asked to read Shakespeare. I, of course, read the Bard's complete works the summer I turned thirteen. And *Romeo and Juliet* is one of my favourites.

Miss Wall walks around the class carrying an armful of books and a small plastic medicine bottle. Everyone receives a copy of the play along with a little yellow pill. I turn it over in my hand. It doesn't take more than a second to find the tiny M&M logo stamped on the shell.

"Shakespeare's plays are arguably the most beautiful works of literature ever written," Miss Wall explains over the noise of crunching candies. "And certainly, the Bard's tragedies are the most stirring and powerful of all his works. But understanding sixteenth-century English can be quite difficult at times. You've all received a special painkiller to help make this a little easier. Now, let's begin."

Brilliant! Our own junior-high version of Mary Poppins. I put the "pill" in my mouth and let the chocolate melt slowly on my tongue, trying to make the sweetness last as long as possible. This class is the highlight of my school day. And it's all because of Miss Wall. Over the past few months, I've been wandering in here during the lunch hour to talk to her. It's as a good place as any to avoid my tormentors. She doesn't seem to mind. In fact, I get the feeling she likes the company. Not once has she ever asked me why I wasn't in the cafeteria with the other kids … but I have a funny feeling that she probably already knows why.

A couple of times I've come close to telling Miss Wall about my problems — the bullying, Mommy's disease, how I'm practically raising my little sisters and brother all by myself. But fear always holds me back. What if she calls Child Services? What if they take us away from Mommy and Daddy?

So, instead, I make sure to keep the conversation light. We talk about books and animals and I tell her which universities I want to attend. I once asked her why she never married and she told me it was because she spends all her free time re-reading the course materials and preparing her lessons.

"I never had much time for dating ... guess you could say that I'm married to my job," she said. I loved hearing that. When I get older, I want to be just as passionate about my career. I pretty much have it narrowed down to two choices. Because I love animals so much, I want to be either a zoologist or a veterinarian. Probably a zoologist.

"You've all heard of Romeo and Juliet," Miss Wall continues as she strolls slowly up and down the aisles. "Before we begin the play, I'd like you all to write down anything you know, or think you know, about the characters. You have five minutes, then we'll discuss."

I extract a pen from my pencil case, flip my binder open to a new page, lean forward, and take a deep breath. I love the crisp, clean smell of fresh paper ... it's so full of promise and potential. Twirling the pen around my knuckles, I stare at the blank page and think about Miss Wall's question.

Who were Romeo and Juliet?

Simple enough. They were two kids I have a few things in common with. I lean over my binder and start writing.

Romeo and Juliet were a pair of tragic teenagers who were mature beyond their years. They became desperate to find a way to escape their unhappy circumstances and came up with a plan. At the end of the play, everyone who'd ever tried to push them around was sorry.

I feel a pair of eyes on me and look up to see Alison Villemere staring at my page from her desk across the aisle. Instinctively, I cover my work with my arm so she can't see what I've written. I don't like to brag, but I'm by far the smartest kid in school. Everybody knows it — which, of course, means that everybody wants to copy off me. But I never allow it. Let them trade their futures for hockey games and shopping malls. Not me. I have a plan to get away from here.

In four years, I'm going to graduate valedictorian and win a full scholarship to the university of my choice. Maybe even three years if I can pull off an early graduation. A scholarship is going to be my one-way ticket out of this abyss.

I look down at the words I've written, figuring with a high degree of certainty that my answer is probably the only intelligent one in the entire class. If I keep working hard, words like these are going to set me free.

tabby

Drip ... drip ... drip ...

The tub faucet in my ensuite has been leaking for weeks. I heard somewhere that in China, a dripping faucet is used as torture. For me it does the opposite — I swear, the dripping saves my sanity. When I'm lying in bed at night, it's the only thing that holds off the awful silence that takes over my house after Nanny Beth goes down to her bedroom in the basement.

The weekends are different, of course. There's always lots of noise then. Dylan and Brandi usually come to sleep over at my house and my parents are always popping in and out. But on weeknights, if Catherine and David are staying out late, I sometimes feel like the silence is going to swallow me alive in my bed. In the past week, they've been out more than normal, sometimes not even making it home at all.

Drip ... drip ... drip ...

As comforting as I find the noise, Nanny, on the other hand, seems to agree with the Chinese. With a sigh, she flips her magazine shut and leans forward on the vanity stool. There's a small frown squatting in the place of her usual perma-smile.

"That faucet's driving me crazy, Tabby. It's been weeks now — haven't you asked your mama to fix it yet?"

Sam, who had been napping at Nanny's feet, opens his sad, brown eyes and stares at me. The skin on his forehead crinkles with curiosity, as if he's wondering the same thing.

"Um, no — not yet," I reply. I'm too embarrassed to tell her the reason why. Lifting my foot out of the bubbles, I stick my big toe into the open mouth of the dripping tap. Nanny waits a moment to see if I need her for anything before opening the magazine back up.

My *mama*. What a joke. In my baby book, it says that my first word was "mama." But that's a big, fat lie. I know that because last year, Nanny confessed to me that she wrote it in there to make my mother happy. I wasn't surprised. After all, that's Nanny's job ... right? And Catherine would never have known the truth, anyway.

Throughout my childhood it was Nanny who made my meals, read me stories, kissed my scraped knees, sung me to sleep, and of course, gave me baths. To this day, she still keeps me company while I soak in the tub. Honestly, after all this time I'd be afraid to take a bath alone. This house is so freaking big, every word out of my mouth makes an echo. Seriously, it's like living in a museum. It's not so bad during the day, but at night it's pretty frightening. I don't know why my parents built such a huge house when they barely spend any time in it. To look important, I guess. I just can't imagine what I would do if Nanny wasn't here.

Last summer, I got the scare of my life when Catherine told me she was thinking about letting her go.

You're almost grown up now, Tabitha, she'd said. *Don't you think that fourteen is too old for a nanny?*

I totally lost it. It was the first time I'd cried in front of Catherine since I was a little kid. Luckily, I was able to convince her to change her mind. It actually wasn't that hard. After I stopped crying and reminded her of all the housework Nanny does around here, she agreed to keep her on for a couple more years.

I look across the room to where Nanny is perched on the stool, leaning over a magazine and twirling her fingers through her long, black ponytail. She's the tiniest grown-up I've ever seen. I think she's, like, four-foot-nine or something like that. She's so small, that, even though she's in her mid-thirties, she still shops at GapKids and can easily pass for a teenager. And it isn't just because of her size, her face looks young, too. Her skin is the colour of honey and just as smooth. When I see old pictures of Nanny holding me as a baby, I'm always amazed at how little she's changed over the years. I swear, she still looks like the same nineteen-year-old girl who'd just arrived from the Philippines to live with us after I was born.

Physically, we're total opposites. From the outside, I'm clearly a Freeman. I have Catherine's thick, brown hair (except hers is dyed blonde now), high cheekbones, and long, thin frame. From David I inherited my square-shaped face and tiger-green eyes. But that's all I got from them, thank God!

I close my eyes and let my head sink down into the warm water. My pulse throbs softly in my ears — a nice little reminder that I'm still alive. I lie like that for a long time, enjoying the sensation of floating — which I'll take over falling anytime. The water slowly turns cool.

Suddenly, I'm startled by the feel of fingers tickling my toes. Giggling, I lift my head out of the water to see Nanny perching on the edge of the tub. Rose-scented bubbles crackle and pop in my ears.

"It's ten o'clock, Tabby," she says softly.

Ten o'clock? Oops. How long have I been lying here?

"I'm going to go down and get ready for bed," she continues, with a yawn. "Have you finished all your homework for tomorrow?"

"Um, yeah … almost," I fib.

"That's my good girl." Her smile is back again, so big it literally seems to stretch from ear to ear. It's wide and warm and infectious and I can't help smiling, too. Nanny takes such good care of me. I'm sure she loves me as much as she loves her own daughter back in the Philippines. When I was younger, I used to bug my parents to bring her over to Canada and raise her as my sister. But Catherine wasn't interested in the idea of raising somebody else's kid. That is, until the year I turned eight and Angelina

Jolie adopted a Cambodian orphan. Catherine thought that was pretty cool. For a week or two there I thought I actually had real a chance at that little sister. But soon enough she lost interest again.

Once, a long time ago, I asked Nanny how she could have left her baby with her parents and moved to the other side of the world. I remember how my question made her wide smile melt into a frown.

"I can't earn very much money in the Philippines," she'd said. "Money can buy a better life and that's something I must do for my daughter."

I didn't really understand her answer at the time. But the next year Nanny's daughter was diagnosed with diabetes, and she asked my parents for a raise in her salary to help with the medical bills. That's when it all began to make a bit more sense.

But still, I know it makes Nanny sad. Sometimes I hear her crying in her room — the noise travels up the air vents from the basement and echoes off my bedroom walls. I tell her how much I love her every day, to help fight off some of her sadness. But as much as I adore her, a small part of me is always afraid: *if she could leave her "real" child, what's to stop her from leaving me one day, too?*

Nanny yawns again. Not wanting to keep her waiting any longer, I pull the plug. The water swirls down the drain, taking the last of the melting bubbles with it. She hands me my robe as I step out of the tub. While I sit on the vanity stool, she puts a towel to my hair and gently rubs it dry, then helps me brush it straight and smooth. When she's done, she kisses my cheek and turns to leave.

"Good night, my dear."

"Good night, Nanny ... I love you."

I hear her slippered feet softly padding down the stairs, and then the door to the basement gently close. A cool shiver runs over my dripping body. I pull my robe tighter and reach down to pat Sam. Still eager for company, I try to tempt him with a game.

"Hey, boy ... wanna play catch?" I ask in my highest-pitched doggie-fun voice.

But Sam's twelve years old and lazy. He plods to my room, heaves himself onto my bed, curls into a ball and, with a loud snort, goes to sleep. After that, the silence begins to creep in — under the door, through the walls, rising up from the floorboards, like smoke from an approaching fire. Before I know it, the silence is here. It fills my ears until the only thing keeping me from screaming is the steady drip of the bathtub faucet.

Dropping my robe on the carpet, I pull on the pajamas Nanny has spread out so neatly on my silk bedspread and scoot in beside Sam. I lie there in my big bed, listening to the dripping tap, staring at the chandelier, and dreading sleep. I struggle to keep my eyes open for as long as possible, trying my hardest to hold off the nightmare I know is coming.

By the way, in case you're wondering, my actual first word was "Nanny."

Lora

Allie, Chelsea, and Cody are all in the tub together. It's a pretty tight squeeze, but they don't seem to mind and it really saves me time. Waves of water slosh onto the floor as they splash, squeal, and giggle.

Just clean it up later, I tell myself, yawning so wide, I can feel the corners of my mouth cracking.

I've been awake since 6:30. That's the time I have to get up and start making breakfast every morning. As usual, I have to wake up the kids, get them dressed and fed, sit Cody on the potty, make sure Mommy has her medicine for the day, and walk everyone to school and daycare. The firefighting community is big on helping each other out, thank God. Usually, one of them or one of their spouses comes to sit in the house with Mommy while I'm at school. Sometimes they'll even make us dinner, which is a huge help. After school I have to pick the kids up, clean the house, and feed the family and the pets. Every day is the same. Only after everyone is in bed do I ever get a chance to study and do my homework. It's a crazy schedule. Sometimes I don't get to sleep until after 1:00 in the morning.

"Shampoo time," I announce, trying to force a bit of pep into my voice. My body is so tired I feel like I can fall asleep right there perched on the edge of the tub. But I still have to wash them, dry them off, dress them, brush their teeth, read them stories and wrestle them into their beds. Oh, and I have to study for a math test tomorrow. Every day I feel like I'm running a marathon that will never end.

I glance at my watch sitting by the sink. It's 8:45 — if I hurry, I can still get a couple hours of cramming in. The thought of turning on my computer makes my stomach cramp up with anxiety. Oh God, I hope there aren't any of those awful emails waiting for me. No matter how many times I change my web account, they still manage to find me. Sometimes their words are so mean and hateful, they make me want to lock myself in my room and never come out again.

"I can do it by myself," says Allie. Eager to help, she takes the shampoo bottle and starts washing her own hair, then Cody's.

"Thanks, cutie," I say. Even though she's only seven, she seems to understand our family's situation and has taken it upon herself to be my little assistant. Squeezing a blob of shampoo into my hands, I lean over Chelsea and vigorously scrub the remains of her brother's lollipop out of her wet curls. They're red, just like mine. We're all redheads in this family. It's actually pretty rare. Only about two percent of the world's population has red hair. And the only animals in the wild with red hair are orangutans, squirrels, and foxes. Oh, and there's a breed of red-haired panda in Asia that lives …

"Ouch! You'we huwting me Lowa!" Chelsea wails, interrupting my thoughts. "Stop!"

I pause, close my eyes, and for a nanosecond actually consider it. Seriously, nothing would make me happier than to end this bath and just let her go to bed with a tangled head full of sticky, grape-flavoured candy. But I just can't do it to her. Even though my own hair is kind of greasy and needing a wash. Gosh, I can't even remember the last time I shampooed it. Two … three … four days ago? There's never any time left at the end of the day to take care of myself. No time, and even less energy. But I know they'll make fun of me if I don't wash my hair before school tomorrow. And believe me, the last thing I want to do is give them more ammunition. They make fun of everything about me — the way my nose turns up, and the way I slouch — which you would do too if you stood a full head taller than every other girl in school — my intelligence, and of course, my advanced vocabulary. I've been teased about my freckles (which cover so much of my body that you can't even tell what colour my skin is), my knobby knees, and once I was even teased about the small, brown mole on my palm.

Gross, Frog-face has crap on her hands!

I take a deep breath and open my eyes. The smell of the apple shampoo is almost fresh enough to wake me up … almost.

"Sorry, Chels," I say, forcing my fingers to slow down.

She frowns at me to let me know that I'm not quite

forgiven. A moment later, however, the frown is replaced by a wide-eyed stare.

"Lowa, why's the watew diwty?"

I look down and see a murky brown cloud spreading slowly through the bath.

Oh my God!! Cody pooped in the tub!

"Everybody out!" I yell, grabbing the girls under their arms and pulling their slick bodies out onto the bath mat. I grab Cody last and plunk him right onto his potty, maybe a bit too roughly because he starts to cry.

Chelsea and Allie stand dripping and shivering on the bathmat while I drain the sewage out of the tub. Cody is still crying. Sure enough, Chelsea joins in too.

"It's okay guys … it's okay," I say, trying to make myself heard over the wailing while I rummage under the sink for the Lysol. I know I'm not convincing because they keep crying. I want to cry, too, but that would just make this worse. Allie tries to help by singing a wobbly version of "Itsy-Bitsy Spider," but for some reason it just makes them cry louder. Out of the corner of my eye, I see our pet rabbit Peter hop by the door to investigate all the noise. But he quickly hops away when he sees the pandemonium in the bathroom. Smart bunny!

"Lora?" a weak voice floats into the bathroom from down the hall. "Whaz going on?"

It's Mommy — the crying must have woken her up. And she's slurring her words again. That's never a good sign.

"Errything all right in there, Lora?"

My eyes take in the scene in front of me ... the sobbing kids, the dirty bathtub, the puddles on the floor.

No, I want to scream. *No, nothing's all right! Nobody understands what I'm going through. I need someone to come and take care of me!*

As much as I want to let those words out, I clench my jaw and hold them in. If Mommy heard that, she would drag herself out of bed and come to check on us — something I know she isn't strong enough for.

No, it's just easier to try and handle it all on my own.

I take a deep breath and wipe at the tears that are welling in my eyes. I remember when my mother was so vivacious and full of life. And now it's like that person is gone forever. I take another deep breath and shout out a big lie.

"Yes, Mommy. Everything's fine!"

I wait for an answer and am relieved when none comes. She's gone back to sleep. Finding energy I didn't think I had, I quickly clean the tub, refill it with fresh water, and stick them all back in. The warm water works its magic and calms the little ones right down. The splashing and giggling begins again. I glance over at my watch and sigh wearily.

9:34.

Dear God — it's going to be another late night.

tabby

To celebrate my fifteenth birthday, David and Catherine make a reservation at their favourite Italian restaurant, La Scalinata, which, of course, is the fanciest one in town. My parents live by the motto: *if it's not expensive, it's not worth it.* If they had asked me, I would have chosen something more casual. But, naturally, nobody asked me. Not that I really care. I'm just excited for my present. I've been looking forward to this birthday for a long time.

This is the year I'm supposed to inherit Grandma's pearl bracelet — the one Grandpa had given to her on their wedding day in the place of a ring. They were living in Poland then, and it was the same bracelet his own grandmother had left it to him when she'd died and it was really, *really* old. The bracelet had meant so much to my grandma. The only times I ever saw her take it off was when she was letting me try it on. I remember loving the way the cream-coloured pearls slid like marbles up and down my small wrist and how, when I stood by the window, the tiny diamonds on the clasp would catch the sun and reflect little pinpricks of light off the walls.

Every time I tried the bracelet on, Grandma would tell me a story about Grandpa. How they got married when they were both just eighteen and after only knowing each other a month. How Grandma was so shy the first year of their marriage that Grandpa used to make up love songs on their piano to win her over. How, after that first year of marriage, the Nazis invaded Poland and they were forced to go into hiding in a neighbour's cellar, where they lived for five years. Grandma's voice always lowered to a whisper when she talked about that time in her life. Like a part of her still worried she'd be discovered if she made too much noise.

Down in that awful cellar, Grandpa had sung the love songs to her in soft whispers so he wouldn't be overheard. She told me that during those long, dark years, that bracelet and Grandpa's songs were her only reminders of the beauty and light that still existed in the world. Those two things gave her the hope she needed to keep going every day until the war was over.

Grandma always cried happy tears when she talked about Grandpa. I wish I'd had the chance to know him, but he died long before I was born. She left me the bracelet in her will and Catherine had promised I could have it when I turned fifteen. Today is the day. Even though it's a cold night, I make sure to wear short sleeves so I can show it off. I can't wait to see it again. I've made myself a promise to wear it every day ... just like Grandma used to when she was alive. Back then, Catherine used to drop me off at her house to get rid of me on weekends when Nanny wasn't working. Grandma always tried her best to make me forget that I was being dumped there. We used to cuddle in her bed with a bowl of popcorn and watch movies for hours. And she always stocked her house with cookies and candy and let me eat as much as I wanted. And she would brush my hair until it shone and braid it just like she wore it when she was little and tell me stories from the "olden days." I miss her so much. She was the only family member I ever had who really, truly loved me. I can't wait to see her bracelet again. It'll be like getting a little piece of my grandma back.

We all arrive at the restaurant separately. Although David offered to pick me up on his way from the office, I refused and took a cab instead. I hate riding in his Bentley. It's so pretentious. Of course, he has to drive the most expensive car anyone in this town has ever seen. It's embarrassing how much he likes to shove his wealth down other people's throats.

Catherine is late, as usual. That means that David and I have to actually talk to each other. Not an easy thing to do, considering the fact that we have nothing in common. My father's a strung-out workaholic. He's spent virtually every waking minute of the last fifteen years building up his business into the most successful law practice in town. Sometimes entire weeks go by when I don't see him. I didn't realize he actually lived in the same house as me until I was six years old.

I stare across the table into the green eyes that are so exactly like mine. He shifts uncomfortably in his seat and glances away. A second later, he opens his mouth to speak, but nothing comes out. He clears his throat, checks his Rolex, and adjusts his tie. I should probably say something and help him out. But I don't. Watching him struggle is sort of fun, in a mean, sadistic kind of way — like torturing a spider by pulling off its legs.

After a minute he opens his mouth again. This time, he comes up with this gem:

"Um ... so how's school going this year?"

I sigh and roll my eyes.

"Like you really care?"

He frowns.

"Believe it or not, I do, Tabitha. Look, I know I haven't been around very much lately...."

I pick up my menu and pretend to start reading.

"Yeah, right ..."

There's a long silence. I glance up and see that his face has turned a bright shade of red and his eyes are bulging with anger.

"Please don't speak to me that way," he whispers, glancing around to make sure nobody is listening. "I'm still your father and I deserve some respect."

I snort and raise my menu up to my face, blocking him out of my view. Suddenly, a rhythmic clicking breaks through the white noise of the restaurant. I don't even have to turn around to know it's Catherine. The sound of her shoes on the tiled floor is a dead giveaway. She always wears the highest heels she can squeeze her feet into. And I mean *always*. Even if she's just heading out to the bank or to the mailbox.

I turn around just in time to see her click up to our table and glide into her seat.

"Happy birthday, darling!" she says, leaning over and kissing the air beside my cheek. Then, reaching into her Louis Vuitton purse, she pulls out a white envelope and hands it to me. I take it and carefully feel around inside the envelope for the bracelet. It only takes a couple of seconds to figure out it isn't there.

"What's this?" I ask with a frown.

Catherine laughs. "It's a cheque, you silly girl! I didn't have time to go to the store. But I thought you'd like this better, anyway. Now you can choose anything you want."

I shake my head. "But ... no ... what about the bracelet?"

Now it's Catherine's turn to look confused.

"Bracelet?"

"The pearl one ... Grandma's. You know, you promised I could have it when I turned fifteen."

Catherine tilts her head back and laughs. "Darling! I'm sure I never made a promise like that. That bracelet is an antique. It's far too valuable to hand over to a child."

"But, she left it to me in her will. She wanted me to have it."

"It's in our safety deposit box for now. You'll get it when you're ready. Maybe when you're twenty."

My chest suddenly starts to hurt. It feels like someone is vacuuming out my insides. Pushing away the pain, I rip the flap of the envelope open and look inside. Catherine isn't joking — it *is* just a cheque. Not even a card. I stare down at the numbers until they turn blurry and I can feel the sting of tears behind my eyes. I bite my lip hard and will them not to fall. No way am I going to let her see me cry!

Shoving the envelope into my coat pocket, I stare down at my shoes while I wait for the tears to evaporate. I can see the outline of my butterfly ankle tattoo through the thin material of my stocking. I got that tattoo last year. Brandi, Dylan, and I snuck off to an ink parlour in downtown Toronto. I didn't ask my parents because I was sure they'd be upset. Tattooing is against our religion. Technically our family is Jewish — even though we don't really practise much. We almost never go to synagogue and my parents didn't seem to care when I dropped out of Hebrew school and decided against a Bat Mitzvah. But still, I was pretty scared of what they would say about the tattoo. It was a total sin in the Jewish religion — something about defacing the body. I was also nervous about catching a horrible disease from the needle since the only place to accept my fake ID wasn't exactly the cleanest tattoo parlour in the city. In fact, the nervousness was worse than the pain of the needle. I snuck home that day feeling like a total criminal.

But that was last winter. Catherine and David still haven't noticed.

Jerks!

When the waiter comes, I quickly scan the menu for the highest-fat food I can find. Damn my mother and her stupid rules! Tonight, I just want to piss her off. I don't even care if I get fat. In fact, maybe that would be a great way to hit her where it hurts the most. I can't imagine anything worse for her than having a fat daughter.

"I'll have the fettucine alfredo, please," I say, staring right at Catherine as I order. "And, could you ask the kitchen to make that with extra sauce? Thanks."

Catherine frowns. That is, she tries to frown. She's had so much Botox injected into her face that it's hard for her to muster up much expression anymore. Talk about "defacing" your body! She thinks nobody knows she's had work done. I've even heard her bragging to friends about her "natural" beauty. But I know better. I've seen her hurrying home to rest after her various peels and injections and treatments. If she's a natural beauty, then I'm Marilyn Monroe.

"And you, madam?" asks the waiter, pencil hovering above his pad.

"Green salad, dressing on the side. And the grilled salmon — no potato, just extra vegetables." Her words are clipped and stern. She's *royally* pissed.

The waiter scribbles the order onto his pad, then turns toward David.

"And you, sir?"

"Veal Marsala with baked potato," he orders, handing back his menu.

Catherine's shooting me a bitchy glare from across the table. I shoot it right back at her. The waiter turns to leave.

"Sorry ... just one more thing ..." I say, holding up a hand to stop him. "Um, I noticed you have a chocolate cheesecake on your list of specials. I'll have that for dessert."

"Certainly," he nods and scribbles some more.

"Á la mode."

Catherine gasps. The waiter spins around and scurries back to the kitchen.

Once he's gone, David clears his throat and pulls at his tie. Over the top of his collar, the veins on his neck are bulging through his skin like long, blue ropes.

"Ahem ... well, Tabitha, as I was saying before ... I know we haven't been around much lately. Unfortunately, it's not going to change any time soon. There's been a lot going on at the office. Some people have been asking to see some of our old files and your mother has been helping me try to sort it all out. And I'm afraid this could go on for a while yet ... just so you know."

I shrug. "So somebody wants to see your files. Why is that a big deal?"

David and Catherine exchange glances.

"It's absolutely not a big deal," he replies, shaking his head. "It's just going to take some time to get everything straightened out."

I watch in amazement as the veins in his neck bulge bigger and bluer until I honestly think his head is going to explode right then and there. Something's wrong. I feel the hair on the back of my neck stand straight up — like a window has opened and a cool breeze has blown over my head.

"You're not in any kind of trouble, are you?" I ask, suddenly serious.

Catherine leans forward and points a perfectly manicured finger at me. "Of course your father's not in trouble," she hisses. "And we're both working our butts off to make sure it stays that way."

"For God's sake, Catherine!" David growls, pounding his fist down on the table.

"I don't get it," I say, shaking my head. "What's going on with you guys?"

"It's nothing for you to be worried about," David replies. "Your mother, as usual, doesn't know what she's talking about. But I do expect you to keep this quiet. This is a private family matter. Don't go talking to your little friends about it."

Now he's pointing his finger at me, too. God, these two really deserve each other.

"And don't talk to Beth about it, either," Catherine adds, reaching for her water glass. "That girl's got a big mouth!" She takes a long sip; the ice cubes clink against the crystal glass like little jingle bells. "I mean, I can't tell you how many times I've come home and found her on the phone, gossiping with her friends," she continues. "Honestly, you'd think we were paying her to talk all day."

I bristle at the mention of Nanny.

"She's not gossiping with friends ..." I shoot back. "She's on the phone with her family in the Philippines. It's hard for her to be so far away ... she misses them."

"I don't care if she's on the phone with the Queen of England. All I know is that if she spent as much time doing her job as she does talking on the phone, maybe our house wouldn't be falling apart."

David runs a hand through his thinning hair and sighs.

"Ladies, please. Can we get back on topic?"

We both ignore him.

"Falling apart?" I reply. "What are you talking about?"

"There's a dripping faucet in your bathroom. Apparently this has been going on for weeks and nobody bothered to tell me about it. I only discovered it when I went looking in your bathroom for my hair dryer."

"That's my fault, not Nanny's."

"No, darling ... she's the employee, not you."

Our meals arrive before I have the chance to reply. God, these two are so selfish! And immature! How can I be related to them? I pick up my fork and twirl my fettuccini around and around until it rolls up into a big, creamy ball. Then I look right at Catherine and shove it into my mouth.

"Mmmmmm ..." I purr, lapping the gooey sauce off my lips. I'm trying my best to pretend that I'm enjoying the pasta, but really it's pretty vile. I haven't eaten anything this fatty in years, and desperately want to hurl it up into my napkin. But that would just make my mother happy. So I keep eating.

Unimpressed, Catherine turns away and ignores me. I hear David's BlackBerry buzz under the table. Pushing his chair back, he pulls it out and starts scrolling through a message. Of course, Catherine takes the opportunity to pull out her BlackBerry and begin typing an email. Suddenly, I feel very alone. That's when the white noise of the restaurant separates and for a moment I can hear every other conversation around me very clearly. Like one of those freaky optical-illusion puzzles that seem jumbled up, but when you look carefully enough you can see the picture hidden in the chaos of swirling colours.

The blonde lady with the glasses at the table beside ours is talking about her day.

The grey-haired fat man at the table behind ours is gushing about some hockey team.

The middle-aged mother in the red turtleneck at the table across from us is laughing and telling a story about one of her kids.

I look around me and see plush chairs, twinkling chandeliers, smooth linen tablecloths, beautiful couples, and nice families. Everything and everyone around us is so civilized and normal ... and we're so pathetic and fake. I look down at the creamy white noodles in front of me and feel sick.

Pushing my plate away, I cross my arms in front of my chest, and scratch at my cold, bare, un-braceleted wrists.

God, I wish Nanny was here.

Lora

Dear God! I'm upstairs changing Cody's diaper when I hear the smoke alarm go off.

BEEEEEEEEEEEEEEEEEEEEEEEEEEEEEEEEP!!!!!!

A moment later, the stench of burning noodles wafts under my nose.

BEEEEEEEEEEEEEEEEEEEEEEEEEEEEEEEEP!!!!!!

Oh no!

Dragging my half-naked brother in my arms, I run down to the kitchen as fast as I can. When I get there, Allie and Chelsea run to my side, holding their ears and looking terrified. The alarm is loud, piercing, and urgent. I scan the room and see the pot of noodles smoking on the back burner of the stove.

BEEEEEEEEEEEEEEEEEEEEEEEEEEEEEEEEP!!!!!!

"It's okay, guys!" I yell above the noise as I lower Cody to the floor, grab the nearest chair, and climb up to where the alarm is installed. A second later, the cover comes off and I yank the battery out. For one blissful moment, the room is silent and then, like a trio of synchronized sobbers, they all burst into tears.

"It's okay …" I say again. But I know I'm not convincing anybody — least of all myself. Dinner is late, the kids are beyond hungry, and I'm on my own with them again — Daddy's on duty at the fire station tonight and Mommy hasn't been out of bed in four days.

I climb back down from the chair, pull the pot off the stove and pour the contents into a strainer. Most of the noodles are burnt and stuck to the bottom of the pot. The whole thing looks like a nest of charred, black worms. I scoop out the few noodles that are still edible into a bowl.

Gosh, what a mess! It's going to take me forever to clean this pot, I think, dumping it into the sink to soak. For a moment I consider throwing it out. But it's our only large pot and I don't have the money to replace it. Even though I make a decent salary at the coffee shop, I always end up giving it all to Daddy to help with Cody and Chelsea's daycare expenses.

"Lora?" whispers a voice.

I spin around and see Mommy standing there, holding onto the wall for support. Her red hair is sticking out from a messy ponytail in a fuzzy cloud of bed-head. Her face is paler than usual and her body is so thin, it makes her nightgown hang like a windless flag. I gasp to see her standing in our kitchen. She hasn't been downstairs in weeks.

"I heard the smoke alarm ..." she says, taking a small, wobbly step forward. "What's going on down here?"

I run to her side to steady her. Her body is childlike and frail and if it wasn't for the bags of fatigue around her eyes, she might have passed for another sister. The little ones follow me, forgetting their hunger in the excitement of seeing Mommy downstairs. They surround us and hug her legs with joy, which of course throws her right off balance. She teeters dangerously until I take her by the arms and shore her up. Suddenly, I hear an authoritative voice speak:

48

"You shouldn't be out of bed. It was just a false alarm. Everything's under control down here — don't worry."

Is that really my voice sounding so stern? I take a deep breath and try to get my irritation under control. I know Mommy wants to help, but she's just making my job harder by coming downstairs.

"Wait here, kids. I'll be right back and we can have dinner."

Immediately, the kids start crying and screaming for Mommy to stay. I pry them off her legs and gently help her back up the stairs to her bedroom which, no matter how often we air it out, always smells of medicine and tears. She's as weak as a kitten in my arms and her legs wobble so much I worry she'll fall down. Trying to keep my brave face on, I put her back to bed. She looks relieved to be lying down again. As much as I want to stay, to cuddle up beside her and go to sleep, I know there's still work to do. I give her a quick kiss and leave.

When I get back to the kitchen, my still diaper-less baby brother hurls himself at my feet and whimpers: "Me hungry … want to eat!"

Right away, the others chime in with their complaints. Even my little assistant Allie can't find a way to help me tonight.

"Where's our dinner?"

"My stomach huwts, Lowa!"

"It's almost ready guys … just settle down *please*," I beg, telling myself that this whole experience is excellent training for my future zoology degree. Honestly, sometimes these little kids are worse than a pack of wild animals.

"Chels ... Al ... maybe you two could help me out and set the table?"

Chelsea stomps her little foot on the linoleum floor and scowls.

"No Lowa! I don't wanna set the table ... I want my skapetti!" she shrieks. I can tell by the crack in her voice what's coming next and brace myself for the worst. Sure enough, a second later she throws herself onto the floor in a full-blown, kicking, screaming temper tantrum. I want to scream too, but I bite my lip and hold it in. This isn't exactly the first time she's done this.

The best way to handle a toddler's tantrum is to ignore it, I can hear Daddy's voice clear as day, spouting advice in my ear.

Ha! Easy for you to say when you're not even here, I think back as I frantically search the fridge for a jar of tomato sauce. I'm sure I saw one last week, lingering somewhere at the back.

"I know you're hungry, but I'm going as fast as I can," I say, trying hard to keep my voice calm. But it's all an act. In reality, I feel like my head is going to explode from the pressure.

When I finally find the sauce, I cover the mushy, overcooked spaghetti with heaps of it, praying they won't notice the burnt noodles underneath. Dinner is cold, but at a time like this I really have no choice.

"Okay, everyone have a seat," I say, dishing the food out into three small bowls. I don't serve any for myself. My stomach is aching, too, but I'm pretty sure it's from stress.

I swear I don't even feel hunger anymore. Kids at school tease me all the time about my body and how skinny it is. But I can't help being an ectomorph. I've tried to eat more, but my stomach is always hurting. Dr. McMullon says it's because of anxiety and if I don't watch out I'll get an ulcer. I don't know how to tell him that getting an ulcer is the least of my worries.

As the kids gather around the table to inspect their ruined food, I notice the dismantled battery sitting on the counter.

Better install it again before Daddy gets home, I think to myself. I know if I don't, he'll have a conniption. In his line of work, he's seen too many houses burn to the ground because there were no batteries in the smoke alarm.

A loud clattering noise breaks through my thoughts. My head whips up to see Chelsea scowling at me and pointing to the floor. My eyes follow the direction of her finger to the spot where her bowl of spaghetti has been overturned in a gory, tomato-y mess. Behind me, I can hear the unmistakable sound of clicking toenails racing across the linoleum and I know the dogs are on their way over to scavenge the dropped food.

"This is yucky, Lowa," Chelsea declares, her face clenched tight like a fist. "I won't eat it. Make something else."

That does it. Turning my head away from the kids, I lower my face into my hands and start to cry. I cry long and hard, until my cheeks are soaked and my mouth is salty with tears. I cry until there's no energy left in my body to cry anymore. I cry desperately, shoulders shaking and heart silently wailing:

Mommy, I need you to be healthy again. I can't do this all by myself. I'm just a kid! Daddy, come home. You're trained to save lives. Please ... why can't you save mine?

tabby

"Where to now, guys?" I ask my BFFs as I drop the change back into my wallet. Hitching my purse up on my shoulder, I collect my new stuff and turn away from the cash register.

I finally cashed my birthday cheque yesterday — it had been sitting in my desk drawer for two weeks, making me sick every time I looked at it. If only I'd had the guts to rip it up in front of Catherine and David that night of my birthday. That would have really got their attention. But it's too late for that now. So instead, I've decided to spend the money fast. Maybe that'll help erase some of the anger I still feel over losing Grandma's bracelet.

"Um ... let's try Roots," suggests Brandi.

"No, let's do Garage," says Dylan.

Because I can, I decide to overrule them both.

"No, I think we should take a break and get something to drink," I say, with a nod toward the coffee shop on the other side of the mall.

"Okay," says Brandi.

"Yeah, I could use a break," echoes Dylan.

Of course they agree. Really, what choice do they have?

I lead the way while the twins follow behind. We make our way easily through the throngs of people. Today's Saturday and, since most of the stores are having sales, the mall is busy. But the crowd opens up to let me through — kind of like in that old movie Grandma showed me when the Red Sea parted for Moses.

When the twins and I get to the coffee shop, we stroll up to the counter to get our drinks. Of course, Tweedle-dum and Tweedle-dee wait to hear what I'm getting before making their orders.

"Large non-fat decaf latte, please," I say.

"I'll have one, too," says Dylan.

"Same for me," Brandi chimes in.

While we fish change out of our wallets and wait for our coffees, I notice a familiar face standing on the other side of the counter. It only takes a second for me to realize that it's Lora Froggett pouring foam into our lattes. The twins notice, too. Dylan pokes my arm with one hand and points with the other.

"Look, Frog-face works here."

"Ha! Maybe she's trying to earn enough money to buy a new wardrobe," laughs Brandi.

I laugh, too.

"At least we can't see her Payless Shoes from this side of the counter," Dylan adds.

Frog-face doesn't look up from the coffee cups, but I can see her cheeks turn a bright shade of pink so I know she's heard us. I don't feel bad. With all the bullying I've seen her take at school, our little comments are nothing.

Suddenly I feel twin elbows poking my arms and I realize that Dylan and Brandi are waiting for me to take my turn. I don't really have anything to gain by putting Lora down, but sometimes I just go along with the rest of them because I know they expect it. And let's face it, she's such an easy target.

"Here," I say, dropping the change from my coffee into the tip jar, "... just a little something extra, so you can splurge on your next trip to Value Village."

With the pennies still ringing against the glass, Lora's face dips down toward the floor and I think for a second that she might actually cry. *Damn, maybe that one wasn't so harmless.* I turn away from the counter before the twinge of guilt that's pricking at my conscience can grow any bigger.

We pick up our cups and take a seat at a nearby table — the only empty one in the shop. It doesn't take long to see why nobody else is sitting there. Some slob has spilled their coffee and left their muffin crumbs all over the place.

"Excuse me, could we get this table cleaned? It's kinda gross," I ask the hairy waiter who's standing nearby. Disgusted, I drop my shopping bags onto an empty chair and sit down.

A girl with green hair comes over to wipe down our table. As she's mopping up the crumbs, she accidently bumps Brandi's arm and tips over her latte. It spills all over the table and floor, just missing her brand-new pink Uggs.

Brandi jumps to her feet and starts to yell at the waitress — who has a funny look on her face, like she's trying to swallow a smile. Brandi calms right down after the waitress promises to bring a new latte.

Beside me, Dylan rips open three packs of sweetener and pours them into her cup. I can hear the chemicals fizzling as they sink into her coffee.

"So, how much do you have left to spend?" she asks, stirring her drink with a little brown stick.

I do a quick mental calculation.

"About a hundred bucks."

The twins smile and rub their hands together with greedy excitement. Shopping is their all-time favourite hobby — especially when they're spending someone else's money.

I turn and look at all the shopping bags balancing on the chair next to me and feel a big, empty hole open up inside my chest. Brandi and Dylan can have this stuff for all I care.

I think about Grandma and how much I miss her and the hole widens so deep that I think it might just suck the rest of me in and swallow me up. Tears prick at the corners of my eyes, but I blink them away. I want to run home, crawl into my safe bed, listen to my drippy faucet and never come out again.

I don't want the crap in these bags. I don't want these parasites for friends. Yeah, we have a lot of fun together, but I don't kid myself. Deep down, Dylan and Brandi are no different from anybody else in my school. I know they only like me because my family's rich. I know they're jealous of my house and my clothes and my parents' status. And I know, without a shred of doubt, that they would stab me in the back the first chance they got.

They aren't real friends ... I know that because the nastier I treat them, the more desperately they cling to me and kiss my ass. A real friend would call you out for being a bitch, tell you the truth about yourself, not put up with any crap.

A real friend would like you for who you are — not what you own.

Lora

"Lora, I need you to restock the stir sticks! *ASAP!*" bellows a voice from behind me.

I don't have to turn around to know that it's Mike. He's my boss at the coffee shop where I work on weekends — a short, stocky college freshman with the loudest mouth, pointiest teeth, and hairiest arms of anyone I've ever met. Mike's on a massive power trip. It's obvious to everyone within earshot how much he enjoys managing an all-female team of adolescent baristas. He loves ordering us around and never says please or thank you for anything. Totally typical alpha male. In fact, if I had to choose a primate subgroup to classify him into, I'd definitely have to go with baboon. Still, I'm careful not to let him know how I really feel. This job is too important.

I've been working here part-time since the beginning of the school year. Daddy watches the kids while I'm gone — unless, of course, he's on duty at the fire station. Then one of the other firefighters' wives comes over to help out. It's only twelve hours a week, but I know the extra little bit I earn here really helps our family. And, even though I'd rather be reading or doing homework, I actually don't mind making moccaccinos and espressos for over-indulged, caffeine-addicted yuppies. It's a nice break from the stresses of home and school.

I've even made a friend here. Her name is Madison, she's sixteen, has green hair, a nose ring, and dropped out of school earlier this year. She's the only person who knows the truth about what's going on with my family.

Next month, we're going to start staying open late on Sunday nights for poetry readings. After half an hour of begging, Daddy agreed to let me stay and work late those nights — on the condition, of course, that I always have a lift home. I worked it out with Madison — on the nights Daddy's at the fire station, she's promised to drive me.

"Did you hear me, Froggett?" Mike hollers. "I need stir sticks now!"

"Okay, sure, right away," I reply, before turning on my heel and hurrying into the supply room at the back of the store.

I re-emerge a minute later with the box of little brown stir sticks in my hands. But I almost drop it when I see what's waiting for me at the front of the shop.

"Oh God!" I gasp.

Three of the most vicious piranhas from my school are lining up at the counter for coffee. Luckily, I spot them before they spot me. There's still time to run. I turn back to the supply room to hide out until they're gone. But Mike sees me and thwarts my escape.

"Let's go, Froggett," he snarls, pointing a stubby finger toward the counter. "I need you at the front now!"

"But ... but ..."

"Move it! We're starting to get lined up here."

Big ape! I want to yell. But, of course, I don't. Instead, with a wave of nervous cramps seizing my stomach muscles, I limp up to the cash register where Madison is taking orders and, as inconspicuously as possible, refill the stir-stick dispenser. That's when I hear the piranhas order their coffees. A cold shiver runs up my spine at the sound of their voices. I know it's them without even looking. They sound confident and careless and there's an underlying laughter behind their words — like they're sneering at the world.

"Three large decaf non-fat lattes — Lor, will you give me a hand with the steamer, please?" asks Madison.

I nod, afraid to speak in case the piranhas recognize my voice. I start up the steamer. It hisses and sputters — like a python with respiratory failure. As I help prepare the coffees, I lower my face, let my hair hang down as a kind of curly red veil and pray they won't notice me. But that just makes Madison suspicious. She knows me so well.

"Hey, something wrong, Lora?" she asks, peering at me as she punches the orders into the cash register. I ignore her and concentrate on keeping my head down and pouring foamy milk into the trio of paper cups. I can feel a cold sweat break out across my body as I top off the last one. It's almost over. *Please God, just let them take their coffees and go!*

And then I hear it. One of the twin piranhas recognizes me. I can't tell if it's Brandi or Dylan, but it doesn't really matter, anyway.

"Look, Frog-face works here."

My heart sinks into my shoes but I keep pouring, pretending not to hear.

Oh please, not here! Please God, just make them go away!

While the other twin laughs and says something mean about my clothes, I slump my shoulders down and curl my chin into my chest, trying to make myself smaller, smaller, smaller.

Please God, just let me disappear!

"At least we can't see her Payless Shoes from this side of the counter," another voice says.

A small fire of shame starts burning inside my chest. It burns so badly I think I might faint from the pain. The fire quickly spreads to my face, making my eyes tear from the heat.

A second later, the sound of pennies hitting glass clatters in my ears.

"Here," sneers the head piranha, "… just a little something extra, so you can splurge on your next trip to Value Village."

Oh God, I hate them ... I hate them ... I hate them ... I hate them ...

I peer up and watch through my hair as they saunter away with their coffees. And then I see Madison. She looks furious and her face is turning as red as mine feels — making for an interesting contrast with her bright green hair. It's probably taking all of her willpower not to say something to those girls. But she knows as well as I do that Mike will fire her on the spot for being rude to a customer. As soon as the last person in line has been served, she turns to me and begins demanding some answers.

"Why on earth did you let them talk to you like that, Lora?"

I shrug and stare at the stack of paper filters on the counter in front of me.

"I don't know why you stand for it," she continues. "I mean, those girls were total bitches. Why do you take that crap?"

I shrug again, hoping my silence will be her cue to drop the subject. But she's persistent.

"That's Tabitha Freeman, isn't it? The hotshot lawyer's kid? And the others ... they go to your school, right?"

I nod. Madison sighs.

"I don't know why you're still there. I mean, you hate school — why are you staying somewhere that makes you so sick? And besides, you're so smart you probably don't even need a diploma."

I shake my head. Ever since Madison dropped out, she's been encouraging me to do the same. But I know dropping out isn't the answer to my problems. They don't give zoology degrees to dropouts.

"You're wrong. I don't hate school — I just hate the people in my school," I reply softly. Then I think about Miss Wall and our lunchtime chats and her Shakespeare pills and have to add: "Well, most of the people, anyway."

A moment later, Mike walks over and hands me a wet rag.

"The customers at table seven have complained that their table is dirty," he says. "Froggett, go clean it!"

I look over. Table seven is where the piranhas are sitting. I let out a small whimper of agony as my stomach begins knotting up again. Reading the pain on my face, Madison grabs the rag from my hands.

"I'll do it, Mike," she says, with a quick glance in my direction.

But he steps in front of her, blocking her way.

"No, I asked Froggett to do it. Are you deaf?"

Madison stares down at him. She's a full head taller than Mike and, unlike me, totally unintimidated by his arrogance.

"No, I'm not deaf. But it's *my* mess — I sat there on my break and forgot to wipe up. So excuse me, but *I'll* clean it."

She steps around him and stomps off to clean the table before he can say another word. *You're an angel, Madison,* I think as I watch her go. I begin wiping down the steam machine, but less than a minute later, the sound of shouting fills the shop. I look back at table seven and see one of the twins yelling at Madison and pointing to her latte splattered all over the floor. A smile tugs at the corners of my mouth and I raise my hand to cover it up. Even though Mike could never prove it, I know in my heart that my friend has exacted her revenge.

That's when one of the other piranhas catches my eye. It's the lead one, Tabby Freeman. She has a look on her face that I know all too well. There's no mistaking it. Despair — with a capital D — is radiating from her so strongly that I can see it all the way over here. For the smallest of seconds, I feel like I'm seeing myself in a mirror. Her pain is so ugly and raw and familiar, I have to look away.

But I can't help wondering: *Tabby Freeman is the richest, most popular girl in the entire town. What can she possibly know about despair?*

tabby

My faucet doesn't drip anymore. I knew it was only a matter of time. Catherine doesn't like anything in her life to be less than perfect.

When I got home from school yesterday, there was a plumber with filthy fingernails and scuzzy jeans kneeling beside my bathtub and packing up his greasy wrench into his dirt-encrusted toolbox.

"Hi there!" he said as I walked in. His voice was gritty and deep and the smell of stale cigarettes hovered around him, stinking up the air in the room. When he stood up, he hiked up his jeans and raked his bloodshot eyes slowly over the length of my body. *Ew!* As upset as I was about losing my drip, I was even more upset about the dirty plumber in my bathroom. Couldn't Catherine have hired somebody a bit cleaner? As soon as he left, I ran to get Nanny and had her help me disinfect the tub.

Without my drip, it was so quiet in my room that night; so quiet, I thought I was going to go crazy. I finally ended up falling asleep listening to my iPod. It helped with the silence, but it didn't keep the dream away. And when Sam woke me up just before my crash landing, the iPod was playing "Fallin'" by Alicia Keys. Is that whacked or what?

Tonight I decide to try something different to fight the silence. Once I'm in bed, I reach for the remote and snap on the TV. *Ah, much better!* Relief falls over me like a warm rain. I rub Sam's ears and yawn. I'm exhausted and sore all over. Every muscle in my body is aching. I think I overdid it at the gym today, but I'm still trying to make up for eating that gross fettuccine alfredo the night of my birthday. My eyelids begin to droop, but I fight to keep them open. I'm afraid to fall asleep, afraid to have the dream again. *What will happen if Sam doesn't wake me up in time?* I wonder.

I miss my drip.

I look over at the clock on my nightstand.

1:03 a.m.

Too late to call the twins. Their mother will have a cow if I wake her up this late.

But maybe they're online.

Switching off the TV, I bounce out of bed, grab my laptop and fire it up. As soon as it's online, I send an IM to Brandi:

Hey B, r u awake?

I wait a minute. There's no reply.

Damn.

I send one to Dylan.

S'up D?

I wait again. Nothing.

I think for a minute and, after a small hesitation, send one to Derek. The end of the term is around the corner, after all. It's time to start giving him some hope.

Hey Der r u there?

I take a long, shaky breath and wait. If he's online, this might turn into an interesting night after all. Suddenly, I hear a bump and my ears prick up.

Are my parents home?

I hold my breath and listen.

A second later another bump ... then another.

Oh no ... what if someone's broken in?

Another bump.

I look behind me and see Sam thumping the mattress with his wagging tail. He's dreaming again. I let out a long breath. Being alone all these nights is turning me into a paranoid freak. Where the hell are Catherine and David? I can't even remember the last time I saw them. Four days ago ... five days ago? I think back to that night at the restaurant.

There's been a lot going on at my office ... some people have been asking to see some of our old files, David had said. For the hundredth time since that night, I find myself wondering who he was talking about. The police? The government? His accountants? Other lawyers? Whoever it was, I'm pretty sure it meant trouble.

That's when I see it — a message waiting for me in my email box. It's from Catherine. I click it open and start to read:

Tabitha,

This is an emergency so pay attention. We've just been tipped off that your father's company is coming under suspicion of billing fraud. I'll explain what that means next time I see you. But for now, you need to know that we'll be here all night cleaning up and getting things sorted out. Whatever you do, do not answer the door. Do not pick up the phone. Do not talk to anyone. We'll explain more when we see you.

And please, don't wait up and don't reply to this message — I'm too busy and there's still so much to do here. And whatever you do, don't tell anyone about this.

Catherine.

I swirl the mouse around in frantic circles. *Under suspicion?* WTF?! How much trouble are those two in? I read the email again. "Billing fraud." What the hell does that mean, anyway? Giving up on Derek, I close my IM, open up Google and type in four words: *Law firm billing fraud.*

I click "search." A second later, my computer comes up with half a million results. I started scrolling through the links. What I read leaves my jaw hanging open. Stories of rich lawyers making off with illegal millions, law firms shutting down, court proceedings, men in suits being hauled off to jail. Oh my God! Has David been stealing from his clients? That would mean pretty much everyone in this town. How much money has he stolen? Who else knows about this?

Don't tell any of your little friends, David had warned.

Don't talk to anyone, Catherine had written.

God, I hate them! Don't they ever care about anyone but themselves? They commit a crime and now they're sneaking around in the middle of the night trying to cover it up? Screw that! They totally deserve to get caught!

Suddenly, I have an idea. A brilliant idea. It's like a light turning on inside my head and in a split second I know what I have to do to get them where it will really hurt the most. No more messing around with stupid pranks like fatty pasta. This time, I'm going to hit a bullseye. Without even the smallest hesitation, with one tiny flick of my finger, I do something that I know will change my parents' lives forever.

Don't reply to this message. I'm too busy, she'd said. That's nothing new. From the day I was born, she's always been too busy for me. So why does it still hurt?

"Fine, Catherine, you get your way," I whisper, with an angry tap of the mouse, I click "forward" instead of "reply." I know my BFFs will know exactly what to do with this information.

```
To: Dylan; Cc: Brandi
Subject: My father's a crook
and my mother's a liar.
```

My chest is tight and I can feel a prickly heat growing under my arms and spreading up my neck. I hold my breath, close my eyes, and click "send."

As soon as the message is gone, I feel a little ball of pain form in the pit of my stomach and slowly creep up and down my entire body. Closing my computer, I crawl back into my bed and switch the TV back on. The next time my eyelids start to droop, I let them close. Tonight, for the first time in years, I don't wake up in a panic. The dream doesn't come.

I think it's because in my real life, I've just taken a flying leap off that tall building.

Lora

Dear God, nighttime in my bedroom sounds like an overrun animal shelter. It's so loud in here that, if I wasn't so constantly tired, I don't know how I'd ever get to sleep.

Buster, our cat, is sleeping in Allie's bed and purring so loudly you'd think he'd swallowed a small engine. On the dresser across the room, the trio of hamster wheels squeak and creak as they spin in circles in the dark. Those little guys run like maniacs all night. It's incredible that, after all that running, they still haven't figured out that they're not getting anywhere. Beside me, the parakeet chirps in his cage. I look over at him and see his eyes shining at me through the dark.

"Go to sleep, Frank … it's late," I whisper. He chirps again, louder this time. I know he's trying to get me to feed him. He learned that trick from the dogs, who also share our room.

I ignore him and pretend to be asleep. That bird is too smart for his own good sometimes. My thoughts skip back to Miss Wall's class today. We discussed the lark and the nightingale scene from *Romeo and Juliet*. Bet you neither of *those* birds were as manipulative and crafty as Frank. I mean, how many other parakeets know how to beg for food?

After the class was over, Miss Wall asked me to stay back for a chat. I knew right away she didn't want to talk about universities or animals. There were two deep lines creasing the skin between her eyebrows — a dead giveaway that something serious was on her mind.

"Everything okay, Lora? You look tired."

I bit my bottom lip and shrugged. The lines in her forehead got deeper.

"Those are some pretty black circles under your eyes," she continued. "Are you sleeping enough?"

My palms started to sweat. I could see in Miss Wall's eyes that she wanted to help. And a big part of me wanted so badly to let her — just tell her all my troubles right then and there. But another part of me — the stronger part — was still too scared.

So I just shook my head and stared at my shoes.

"Please, Lora, if there's anything you want to tell me ..."

"No, I'm fine," I'd said, keeping my head down so she wouldn't see the truth in my eyes. I heard Miss Wall sigh.

"All right, Lora. You can go now."

And just like that, my chance was gone.

On the other side of the house, the rhythmic sound of Chelsea's snoring buzzes through the thin walls. My little sister is louder than all the animals combined. She snores so loudly it makes my bed vibrate. And she isn't even in the same room as me. We've had her checked out twice by Dr. McMullon, but even he couldn't figure out how or why a five-year-old child would be snoring like an overweight middle-aged man. The snoring freaks out all the animals, so they all have to sleep in my room. Thank God her snoring doesn't seem to bother Cody or he would want to sleep in my room, too. As it is, there's barely any room left to breathe in here.

Since there's no place for a proper bookcase, the floor next to our dresser is piled up high with books by all my favourite authors: Shakespeare, Hemingway, Steinbeck, the two Margarets (Atwood and Laurence), Rowling, and Dickens, of course ... his writing about kids in workhouses really strikes a chord with me. I treasure my books and would rather keep them in the closet where they're less likely to get stepped on, but there's no room in there, either. It's so crammed with clutter and junk that there's barely enough room for our clothes — which isn't such a bad thing because most of them are dirty, anyway. The laundry bin at the foot of our bed is an overflowing volcano of stinky clothes; a malodorous reminder of all the housework I've fallen behind on.

Trying to muffle Chelsea's snoring, I turn over in my bed and pull my comforter up over my ears. I can feel eyes on me and I know Frank is still staring.

Allie turns around and mumbles something in her sleep. I can hear her breathing, deep and slow. I turn my head to look at her. Her coppery curls are messy and damp with night sweat. Reaching my hand out across the bed we share, I brush her bangs gently out of her face.

When they're quiet and sleeping, it's so much easier to love these little guys. Sometimes I feel like I'm their real mother. And, even though we all know Mommy is nearby, I think they feel the same way about me. Thank God, so far none of them have had an issue with bullies. Allie's in grade two now and there hasn't been even a hint of trouble. I don't know what I'd do if any of them had to deal with problems like mine.

Her little arm flops across my shoulder as she tosses onto her back. I hear her sigh in her sleep like she's having a nice dream. I turn and look at the clock.

1:03 a.m.

I think about all the things other kids my age might be doing right now. Staying out late with friends, talking on the phone, going to parties, hosting sleepovers, having fun, smiling and laughing … not a care in the world. And a piranha like Tabby Freeman? Would she be sneaking out with one of the pit bulls? Probably. For me, the idea of dating is a foreign concept. And the thought of having a boyfriend is completely inconceivable. Even if I had time for one, every boy at my school is an enemy. And every girl, too, for that matter.

There are times when I wish more than anything I could do normal, teenaged things like other kids. But I know that's never going to happen. Even if I had friends, I can't have them over to my house. Mommy needs it to be quiet here so she can rest. And anyway, what would I do with my little brother and sisters if a friend ever wanted to come over and hang out? And how would I have a sleepover in this crowded room? Where would I put an extra person? Under the birdcage? No, there'll be no sleepovers for me. My childhood is officially over.

I flip over onto my back and stare up at the ceiling. For the first time in my life, I notice the shape of my room. It's a perfect square. A small square box crammed inside a slightly bigger box — this house. Suddenly the walls dip inwards and I realize in one awful moment that I'm really no different than any of these animals in their cages. I am *just* as trapped as them. And I'm spinning my wheels harder then those hamsters.

In that moment, the room darkens like a shadow has fallen over the house. Tears roll down my face and into my hair. Some drops manage to make it to my ears where they form little saltwater pools. I close my eyes as the burden of my life comes crashing down from above, pinning me to the mattress with a weight heavier than a thousand cruel jokes.

tabby

Dylan and Brandi did exactly what I knew they'd do and sent the incriminating email out to everyone in their address books. Word spread really fast. It only took two days for the police to make an arrest. The next morning, the story was the headline in the local newspaper.

When I picked our copy up off the front porch, David's bright orange prison jumpsuit was the first thing I saw. Next was his unshaven face, flooded with shame. I'd never seen him look that way before. I stared at the photo for a full minute before noticing the headline.

Local Businessman Arrested for Fraud

Then I started to read:

> Yesterday, police raided the office of the town's most prestigious legal firm, Freeman Law. Officers seized all the files and computers in the building and temporarily shut down operations

pending the completion of their investigation.

David Freeman, president and CEO of the firm, has been charged with multiple counts of fraud, obstructing justice, and destroying evidence. His wife, Catherine Freeman, is also being questioned on suspicion of destroying evidence.

The firm's fifty-two employees have been suspended without pay and are all expected to co-operate with the ongoing investigation.

After spending the night in jail, Mr. Freeman will be arraigned in court this morning and, according to sources, is expected to be released on $25,000 bail. Outside the courthouse yesterday, he spoke to the press briefly.

That's as far as I got before my vision blurred. Once I started crying, I couldn't stop. After a minute, I heard a gasp from behind me and suddenly Nanny was there, tearing the paper out of my hands and pulling me into the house.

"Tabby, what are you doing?"

Sobbing, I clung to her little body and tried to think of an answer. Why *was* I crying? I hated him, didn't I? He deserved whatever he got. Hell, I practically turned him in myself!

But something about seeing my own father handcuffed and wearing an orange prison jumpsuit was surprisingly traumatic. Nanny must have realized that because, before my tears were even dry, she gathered up the newspaper and threw it into the recycling bin. But it was too late to erase what I'd seen — the image had been tattooed onto my brain.

I ran upstairs to my bedroom and, with Sam at my side, watched from my window for Catherine and David to get home from the courthouse. Unfortunately, the first ones to come were the media. I watched in shock as they pulled up in those ugly grey vans with the satellite dishes mounted on top and surrounded our house with their cameras and microphones.

Next came the police. Just hours after David's arraignment, a squad car pulled up into our driveway and two officers stepped out. Dodging the reporters, they charged right up to our front porch and pounded on the door knocker.

"Open up!"

Leaving my window, I ran downstairs to see what they wanted. As I swung open the door, I could see an army of cameras pointed at me. My stomach dropped.

"H-how can I help you?" I asked, trying my best to keep my voice from shaking. But the officers didn't say a word. They just flashed a search warrant in my face and pushed their way past me; their heavy, black boots scuffing up our marble floors. I was amazed at how rude they were. I couldn't remember anybody ever treating me that way before.

It took the officers less than an hour to seize all the computers in our house — including my own laptop. That really freaked me out! *Holy crap!* Were they going to find out that it was me who leaked the information? Would I get arrested, too? My knees felt weak. What would happen if Catherine and David discovered that it was me who told on them?

As soon as the police left, I went back up to my room to watch for my parents. When David's Bentley finally pulled up, reporters and photographers swarmed the car and set off a storm of flashbulbs in their eyes. With their hands covering their faces, my parents elbowed their way through the frenzy and ran inside the house. Sam and I tumbled down the stairs just in time to see them deadbolting the front door.

"David, help me lock all the windows and doors," Catherine yelped. "And Beth, I want you to close all the curtains and shutters! I don't want any of those photographers out there getting our picture."

When I heard that, I almost laughed out loud. Thankfully, I was smart enough to hold it in. Before all this happened, Catherine would have killed to have her picture taken by the press. Two years ago when my parents took me to the Toronto Film Festival, I remember how she would wear dark sunglasses and walk really fast past all the celebrity hotspots, hoping the paparazzi would think she was someone worth photographing. Man, things were really changing!

As David and Nanny carried out their orders, our house slowly morphed into a virtual prison for four. When the lockdown was complete, Catherine gathered us together and spelled out our sentence. Until the media frenzy calmed down, none of us could leave the house, open a window, or even pull back a curtain. We could make outgoing calls, but we had to stop answering the phone in case reporters were trying to get to us. Nanny was put in charge of screening all calls.

"But what about school?" I asked.

"You can miss a few days," Catherine replied.

And that was that. We were trapped like animals in a cage. All of us. For the first time I could remember, my parents had nowhere to go and nothing but time on their hands.

We hunkered down in our hideout. David spent all day in his monogrammed bathrobe and slippers. He gave up shaving and, from the looks of his eyes, I think he stopped sleeping, too. With every day that passed, his beard got bushier and the circles under his eyes got darker until he started to look like some kind of psycho-freak caveman. He spent most of his time pacing from room to room in whispery phone conversations with his lawyer. His brown leather slippers swished loudly as he marched back and forth across the marble floors, speeding up whenever he got agitated. When he wasn't on the phone, he was sitting on the couch in front of the TV with his eyes glazed over like he wasn't really watching the screen.

Catherine wasn't looking much better. For the first time that I could remember, she stopped wearing makeup and high heels and I could see the stress showing through her skin in little lines on her forehead and under her eyes — proof that not even Botox could fight off the pressures of a federal indictment. But that wasn't the only change in her. Even though I was pretty sure she had never lifted a mop in her life, suddenly cleaning became her passion. And the really weird thing was that the house wasn't even dirty — like, at all. But there she was on her hands and knees scrubbing the already-clean floors. It was like aliens had come overnight and swapped her with a completely different woman.

"Come on, Beth!" she called to Nanny as she was waxing the hardwood in the main floor office. "Make yourself useful and give me a hand here!"

She had to be having some kind of a psychotic breakdown. Or maybe this was just her way of coping with being trapped at home — which I knew was the last place she ever wanted to be.

Holy crap, were my parents losing their minds?

The last thing I wanted to do was hang around and find out. But really, what choice did I have? I thought about calling someone and begging them to sneak me out. But who could I call? Definitely not Dylan or Brandi! Once, in a fit of desperation, I picked up the phone and started to dial Derek's cell, but hung up before it started to ring. There was no way I wanted him to come here and see how messed up my family was.

As the hours passed into days, the fridge and the cupboards slowly emptied out. But since nobody could go out to the grocery store to restock, we just made do. With the windows closed up, the house was eerily dark. We floated around in it like ghosts. Nanny went about her job silently, working in the shadows and trying to stay as invisible as possible in order to avoid any more of Catherine's cleaning fits.

As for me, I kept waiting for some kind of emotional meltdown from David and Catherine. An explanation ... an apology ... an accusation about the email I sent out. Something. But it never came. As usual, they were just too wrapped up in themselves to notice me. A couple of times I came close to asking them how they could have done such a terrible thing — stolen from everyone in town and then lied about it. But for some reason I couldn't get the words out. Maybe I was in shock. Or maybe I was developing a severe case of rickets from the lack of sunlight in my life.

This darkness was really hard to handle and the air reeked with the chemically "fresh" scent of cleaning fluids. By the third day I was craving sunlight as badly as a starving man craves food. It was unnatural to be living shut away from the world. For the first time in my life, I began to feel an awful sense of claustrophobia. Finally, I couldn't stand it anymore. One afternoon while my parents were both downstairs, I snuck up to my room, pulled my curtain open a couple of inches and peeked out my window. I just needed to feel the sun on my face for a couple of minutes.

From up there, I had a great view of what was going on below. The media were still camped out on the street, but their numbers were definitely shrinking.

Closing my eyes, I let the light soak into my skin and thought about Grandma and Grandpa. They'd been on my mind a lot during those dark days. It was so hard to imagine how they spent five years hiding in that cellar during the war. And here I was going crazy after four days! More then ever, I wished Grandma were still alive. She'd be able to help us all through this mess — she'd been through so much worse in her life.

Then yesterday, after five days of imprisonment, the principal of my school called and told Nanny that unless I had a doctor's note I had to go back to class. I actually didn't mind. I thought it would be a relief to get out of the darkness.

So this morning after breakfast is over, I push through the last of the reporters and walk back to school. At first, kids just stare like I'm a freak or something. Teachers stare, too, but at least they're polite and try to hide it a bit better. But little by little, I begin to sense everyone's anger. I can feel their eyes on me as I walk down the hall to my first class. And I can hear the hush and hiss of their whispers as I pass their lockers. I try not to let it bother me, but that gets harder as the day goes on.

In my morning gym class, I'm the last one picked for teams. At lunch, I sit alone in the cafeteria, deflecting dirty looks from everyone who passes by. Finally, when I can't take it anymore, I get up and move to Derek's table. I'm kind of hoping that he'll be a gentleman and stand up in my defence. He does stand up — and without a word, walks as quickly as he can to another table. I'm mortified beyond belief.

On my way back to my locker, I spy Brandi and Dylan ahead of me in the hall. When they see me coming, they start to giggle and turn the other way, whispering to each other and pretending like they don't even know me. I walk past them with my head held high. So much for my BFFs! It's weird, but even though they totally cut my family down, I really can't blame them for it. After all, I sharpened the knife and handed it to them myself.

After that, things really turn ugly. "Thief!" someone hisses at my back as I walk into my math class. I speed up and pretend not to hear. But inside I'm dying. I've been the centre of attention my whole life ... but not this kind of attention. I'd expected my parents to be under attack when that email went out. But I never considered that I would be, too. With the click of a mouse, our entire family has turned into public enemy number one.

As I trudge home from school, I make myself a promise:

No matter how bad it gets, I won't ever let them see me cry.

Back at home, the emotional meltdown I'd been waiting for finally happens. But in the end, it's not my parents who break down. After dinner, there's a small knock at my bedroom door and when I answer it, Nanny Beth falls into my arms, weeping and shaking.

"What's wrong?" I ask, suddenly scared. "Are you hurt?"

"No ... but I'm worried, Tabby," she whimpers. "I'm worried about my job."

My breath catches in my throat.

"Why? They didn't say anything about firing you, did they?"

"No, but I know it's only a matter of time ..." she says. "They won't be able to afford to keep me with everything that's going on. And then what will I do? My daughter — I have to send money for her! She's counting on me! Tabby, what will I do if I lose my job? Where will I live?"

Oh crap! I hadn't thought of that! She looks so scared — and it's all my fault. The guilt I feel is so powerful that I can't even bring myself to look at her. Instead, I hug her and tell her not to worry.

"You'll always have a home here. I won't let them fire you."

But that's a lie. If David and Catherine go to jail, I know I can't protect her. Hell, I won't even be able to protect myself. I put on a brave face for Nanny, but deep down inside I'm petrified. The carefully stitched pieces of my life are rapidly unravelling. More than anything, I wish I could take that email back.

At night, a new nightmare haunts my dreams. I'm not falling anymore. This time, I'm standing alone on an empty sidewalk, frozen with panic as the tall building from my old nightmare comes crashing down on top of me.

Lora

Eleven.

That's how many times this week I've made it down the main hall unscathed. It's definitely a record. Thank God, they aren't paying attention to me anymore. It's like I've become invisible or something. Now the piranhas and the pit bulls are devouring one of their own instead.

Everyone in school is talking about what Tabby Freeman's parents did. They're saying that her father stole over five million dollars from the people in our town. And that he's going to be disbarred. Maybe even sent to prison.

And it's not just at school. The whole town is heated up over the scandal. Even Daddy, who normally never listens to gossip, mentioned it when he picked me up after the coffee shop poetry reading last Sunday night.

"Don't you go to school with that Freeman girl?" he asked, gripping the steering wheel awkwardly in his huge hands as he manoeuvered the car though the parking lot. Despite myself, I had to smile. Daddy's such a big guy, it's always comical to see him confined in the small space of a car. He looks wedged in — like you'd have to pry him loose with a crowbar to get him out.

"Yeah, I know her. She's in my grade," I replied.

Daddy shook his head and let out a long, low, monotone whistle.

"Man, that family's got a lot of problems."

I just nodded and stared out the window. I mean, really … what could I say? I don't know if any of it's true or not. All I know is that I'm happy to be left alone. Some teenagers dream of being popular in high school. But total obscurity is all I ever wanted … to blend into the background. To be wallpaper.

I push open the door to my English class and quietly sneak inside. Miss Wall hasn't arrived yet, so I sit down, open up a book and start to read while I wait for class to start. A minute later, Tabby Freeman comes in. I watch in shock as she slides into the seat beside me, graceful as a cat.

What's she doing? Normally, she likes to hang out in the back with all the other piranhas and pass notes and send text messages away from Miss Wall's nearsighted eyes. Why is she sitting next to me? I don't want her next to me! I like being invisible and I want to stay that way! With all the rumours going around about her family, having Tabby Freeman sit beside me isn't going to help me maintain my wallpaper status.

I twirl a red ringlet around my finger and watch her out of the corner of my eye. She looks smaller and thinner than usual. Kind of deflated — like someone has let all the air out of her ego.

Little by little, the other kids start to fill up the seats. So far so good — the piranhas are keeping to themselves. But then trouble appears in the form of a gap-toothed jock wearing a hockey jersey — Todd McGurk. On his way to the back of the class, Todd pauses in front of Tabby's desk and snaps his thick fingers in her face.

"Hey, my dad wants his money back," he says.

Laughter bounces around the classroom. My stomach twists into a tight knot. I peek over the top of my book and notice Tabby turn away from Todd, as if she's been hit. He leans across her desk and snaps again, just inches from her nose

"Did you hear me? I said your father's a dirty crook."

"Shut up, Todd!" she hisses, trying to shove him away. But he doesn't move. I'm horrified. Todd and Tabby used to be friends.

"He paid for that big house of yours by stealing money from our families."

When she doesn't reply, Todd reaches down and sweeps her big leather purse off the floor. He pulls it open and starts rifling through it.

"Where's my money? I want it back!"

A moment later, he finds her wallet and holds it up for everyone to see.

"Hey look!" he shouts, dropping the empty purse to the floor. "Let's see if the bitch has a credit card!"

Jumping to her feet, Tabby releases a torrent of expletives so shockingly crude that I immediately feel myself transform into a mortified tomato. For that brief moment, I actually forget that she's the one being bullied. With her long fingernails bared like an animal's claw, her hands swipe through the air as she tries to retrieve her wallet. But Todd's taller and he holds it over her head, just out of her reach. Cheers erupt around the room. The knot in my stomach tightens. *What's going on? This guy is mugging Tabby and they're egging him on?*

"Give it back!" she shrieks. "Or so help me I'll ..."

"You'll what?" spits Todd. "Tell your father?"

Tabby's face flushes pink and her eyes turn a bright, fluorescent shade of green. I can tell she's holding back tears. I want to say something to help her. But I'm too scared to utter a sound.

Suddenly, I hear the classroom door slam. I spin around to see Miss Wall standing by the entryway, hands on her hips and eyes ablaze. I've never seen her look angry before. She marches over, plucks Todd up by the collar of his shirt and directs him to the nearest empty desk.

"Take a seat, Mr. McGurk!" she says, pushing him down onto the chair. "It's time to settle down and get started."

On her way back, she stops by Tabby's desk to return the wallet and places a gentle hand on her shoulder. Sympathy oozes from her kind face.

"Are you all right, Miss Freeman?"

Tabby flinches away from Miss Wall's hand and doesn't reply. For the rest of the class, she sits there in stony silence. When the bell rings at the end of class, Tabby leaps from her chair and hurries out the door. Though I've never liked her, I feel sorry for her as I watch her go. Her shoulders are hunched over and her head is down. She looks like — what's that animal with the round shell called? Oh yeah, an armadillo. She looks like an armadillo trying to scuttle away to safety.

I gather up my books and follow her out. For the first time in my life, I'm not the one getting picked on. So why do I feel so bad about it?

tabby

My life is crumbling to pieces around me. At school, the kids are getting meaner by the day. Last Wednesday, there was spit dripping down the front of my locker when I arrived in the morning. Totally disgusting! I complained to the principal, but it didn't do any good because I found more spit on my locker today.

At home, David and Catherine are fighting for their lives and Nanny's perma-smile has been replaced with a wide-eyed look of fear. And as for me, I'm a total wreck. I don't sleep much anymore. Night time is when *they* come — the anonymous voices yelling and cursing our family from the shadows of the street. The first night, they threw eggs, tomatoes, and garbage at our house and I hid under my blanket with Sam. The second night, they threw rocks. When a large stone shattered my bedroom window, I picked up Sam and ran screaming down to Nanny's room to hide out until morning. As soon as Catherine and David called the police, the attacks stopped. But I'm still too scared to sleep much. Night after night, I lie awake in my bed listening for noises and waiting for them to come back. While I lie there, I think a lot about what

I've done to this family. The ball of pain that began in my stomach after sending that email is still there — and it's growing bigger with every passing night. My awful secret is rotting inside me. I know the only way to get rid of it is to do something drastic.

I know I have to confess.

This morning, before I get out of bed, I stare at the ceiling and promise myself that this will be the day I tell Catherine and David the truth about the email. My whole body is twitching with nerves as I walk down the stairs to meet them for breakfast. It's early in the morning, but they're already in the kitchen — sipping their coffees and whispering about the huge mess their lives have become. I sit down at the table, my chest so tight I can barely pull in a breath.

"Good morning, darling," Catherine says, passing me an empty cereal bowl and spoon. Her eyes are glazed over with exhaustion, but she manages a weak smile. I find myself smiling back. Funny, for the first time in my life, I'm kind of getting used to eating meals with Catherine and David. Lately, we've been starting to feel a little bit like a real family — a highly dysfunctional family, but still. Will it all fall apart when I tell them about the email?

All through breakfast, the secret sits in my belly churning and rumbling to get out. But whenever I open my mouth to start talking, the words rise up and catch in my throat. How can I admit what I did? I don't even know where to start. What will they do when I tell them that I ruined their lives? Will they scream at me? Ground me for life? Kick me out of the house? Disown me?

Breakfast comes and goes and I don't say a word. On my way to school, I decide to write my confession down. I normally hate writing, but it's the only thing I can think of to help me sort out my thoughts. So when I get home, I stretch out on my bed with a notepad and pen. Instead of working on that lame poetry assignment for English, I scribble out my confession.

Catherine, David, I have something to tell you. You don't know this, but I'm the reason you got arrested. I told everyone your secret. Everything that's happening right now is my fault.

Halfway through, I begin to cry. My tears dot the page and blur the ink, but I keep going. Sam scooches across the bed and starts licking the tears from my cheeks. "Thanks boy," I say, grateful for his loyalty. He's the only one in this house who hasn't turned into a total head case these past few weeks. When I'm done writing, I read my script over and over, memorizing it like homework.

"Tonight at dinner — that's when I'll tell them, okay, boy?" I say to Sam — as if saying it out loud to a dog will give me the guts to go through with it. For an answer, he rolls over onto his back and whines for me to rub his belly.

That night in the dining room I'm still too nervous to tell them — even with the whole speech planned out.

Before I know it, the meal is over; Nanny has cleared the table and is cleaning up in the kitchen.

Come on, Tabby! the little voice in my head screams. *Don't be such a chicken! Do it now!*

Realizing that my chance is slipping away, I push my seat back from the table and open my mouth. This time, the words rise all the way to my lips. But before I can start, Catherine cuts in with a speech of her own.

"Darling, as you know, this has been a difficult time for our family," she says. I can tell from the stiffness of her voice that her words are just as rehearsed as mine. "Your father and I have been under a lot of stress," she continues. "We've been talking a lot over the past few weeks and we've agreed that we need to make some changes. And ... well ... one of the first things we have to do is to start cutting back."

I frown, feeling my confession slide back down into my stomach. "What do you mean? On what?"

My parents exchange glances. "You tell her," Catherine says with a sigh. She turns her head and starts wiping at her eye, as if there was a speck of dust or something stuck in there. It's not mascara — I know that for sure. She hasn't worn any makeup since the night of the arrest. With a nod, David picks up where Catherine has left off. His beard is fully grown in now, making him seem more like a lumberjack than a businessman.

"What your mother means is that we have to start cutting back on our finances," he explains. "As you know, the office has been shut down indefinitely. We have no money coming in right now. And, unfortunately, we're not the only ones. Because of these charges, there are a lot of people who've found themselves out of work. Most of them have been with the firm from the early days when we were just starting out. They've been very loyal to us over the years and I'd like to offer them some severance pay."

I roll my eyes. "Yeah, right. Since when do you care so much about anyone else?"

He ignores my comment and keeps talking. His voice has changed in these past few weeks — he's lost that hard, angry edge.

"We also have mounting lawyers' fees and we're really beginning to feel tight for cash. It's time to start thinking about the future and that's going to mean some changes around here. Some pretty drastic changes."

"Oh no ... like what?" I don't even try to hide the sarcasm in my voice. I mean, how can anything be more drastic than David getting hauled off to jail and Catherine ditching her makeup?

He takes a deep breath and lets it out slowly.

"Your mother and I have decided that we're going to put the house up for sale in the next few weeks. And we're going to sell one of the cars and cancel our trip to Italy this summer. And ..." he pauses and turns his ear toward the kitchen. We can all hear the sound of water running and dishes clattering as Nanny cleans up from the meal. With a sad shake of his head, David lowers his voice to a whisper and says, "... I'm sorry to tell you this, but we've decided to give Beth her notice. We'll tell her next week and of course, she'll get a generous severance, as well."

"What?"

I stare at them in shock. My eyes jump from his face to hers. They stare back at me, looking like a pair of wounded animals. Clearly, this is no joke.

"We're letting Nanny Beth go," he repeats. His words hang in the air like a bad smell. Suddenly, I feel something inside me snap. My mouth springs open and all the pent-up anger I've kept bottled inside for so many years comes erupting out of me.

"Shut up! How can you do this to her? This isn't *her* fault!" I can feel my voice swelling into a scream as I point to the kitchen. "She's got a daughter to support back in the Philippines — a sick daughter. Did you even know that? How can you treat her like this? You two are the criminals here!"

They make me so sick. I want to hurt them, kick them, hit them, make them cry. I clench my fists as my eyes dart around the table, looking for something valuable to throw. Out of desperation, I pick up a small crystal vase and hurl it down onto the marble floor. Catherine jumps in her seat at the sound of the smash. She looks like a frightened child. But still, I keep going.

"You're both so selfish! You've never given a damn about anybody but yourselves!"

The water in the kitchen stops running and I know Nanny is listening, too. But I can't stop myself. Even though my throat is starting to hurt, I keep going. I'm like a bottle of soda that's been shaken too hard.

"Why did you do it, anyway? Did we really need money so badly that you had to steal it? Look at this house! It's the biggest one in town and you've barely even lived in it. And you own the flashiest car in town and you don't even like to drive! You two are whacked! I'm glad they arrested you! You deserved to get caught! I hope both of you rot in jail!"

The flames on the dinner candles flicker with the force of my screams. And the louder I scream, the quieter they get. Catherine looks like someone has slapped her across the face, which gives me a nice feeling of satisfaction. But when she lowers her head into her hands and starts to sob, I feel a surprising twinge of regret. For a second, my anger disappears. I stop screaming and pull in a long, shuddery breath as a thought flashes through my mind.

Oh my God — is it actually possible that maybe I'm being the selfish one here?

But when David walks over with his arms outstretched and tries to give me a hug, I feel my fury flare up again.

"No! Don't touch me!" I shriek, pushing him away. "I hate you both!" I fire them a look of pure poison and jump up from my chair. Crunching through the mess of broken crystal, I stomp off to my room and fling myself onto my bed.

Five minutes later, there's a soft knock at my door. I know it has to be Nanny Beth, coming to comfort me and to find out what had happened.

"Come in," I say, taking a long, slow breath to calm myself down. I don't know if I'm ready to talk, but I know her smile and gentle voice will help to soothe me as always. But to my shock, it's not Nanny who walks through the door.

It's David.

I can feel my body tense up again, getting ready for another fight. But before I can say a word, he sits down at the foot of my bed and begins to speak. His body is trembling so much that I can feel the tremors in the mattress springs. It's almost like there's a miniature earthquake happening inside him. I force my anger down for a minute and hear him out.

"I'm so sorry, Tabitha," he begins. "Every single thing you said down there was true. Your mother and I *have* been selfish. And you've suffered from it more than anyone. But I want all that to change. I've had the chance to do a lot of thinking over these past few weeks. In fact, the night I spent in that jail was a revelation of sorts. It forced me to start re-examining my character, my priorities, my values. I've begun to understand that I've made a lot of mistakes in my life. And by far, the biggest mistake I've made has been messing up my relationship with you."

He looks at me with those eyes that are so exactly like mine, and for the first time in my life I don't totally hate him.

"I want to be a good father," he continues. "In fact, I *know* I can be a good father. But you have to be willing to give me a chance. I wouldn't blame you if you said no … but maybe you could just think about it? We could start all over again — be a real family. That's what your mother and I are both hoping for …"

David's voice fades away to a whisper and his eyes fill with tears. I sit there on my bed, too shocked to say anything. I've never seen my father cry before. What is he doing? Why is he being so nice to me? I don't want to forgive him. That would be letting him off too easy. I want him to keep hurting.

"So it's all true, then?" I ask, keeping my voice stony and cold. "You really did steal from all those people?"

He closes his eyes and nods.

"When I started the law firm, I was desperate to succeed and I did some terrible things back in those early years to get the business off the ground. I lied and I cheated and I stole. But that was a long time ago. I've changed my ways since then. For the past five years, I've been walking the straight and narrow — making an honest living. Unfortunately, that doesn't erase the mistakes I made before. And those mistakes are what I'm paying for now."

He hangs his head. The room swells with an uneasy silence. Suddenly, my own confession rises to my lips. Before I know what's happening, it flies out of my mouth and attacks David.

"I betrayed you and Catherine. It was me."

"What?" He lifts his face to meet mine. His eyes are wide and lines of confusion slash across his forehead. My well-rehearsed script disappears from my head as the hateful words tumble from my lips.

"I spread an email. I called you guys liars and crooks and made sure it got around town. That's why the police arrested you when they did."

I hold my breath and wait for him to get angry, to start screaming and swearing at me. This *has* to make him angry now, doesn't it? But David shakes his head and holds up his hand.

"Please stop, Tabitha … I know all about the email and so does your mother. It's okay."

It takes me a couple of seconds to process his words. Once I do, a rush of emotion comes over me. It's so powerful that it knocks the breath from my lungs. With a gasp, I lower my face into my pillow and begin to cry like a baby. This time, when I feel my father's arms around me, I don't push them away.

Lora

I know it's going to be a beautiful day even before I wake up this morning. I can see the sunlight shining through my eyelids, calling me away from my dreams. And the birds outside my window are singing a little bit louder than usual, as if they're trying to stir me out of bed. When I finally open my eyes, I see beams of warm, dusty sunlight pouring into my bedroom and I know that spring has finally arrived.

When I get downstairs to start breakfast, Daddy is standing in the kitchen tinkering with the coffee pot. I'm so shocked to see him that I let out a little scream.

"Daddy!" I gasp, clutching at my chest. "What are you doing here?"

He throws back his head and lets out a deep, throaty laugh.

"I thought I lived here. Good morning to you, too, Lora-loo."

"No, what I mean is … why aren't you sleeping? Is something wrong?"

Daddy just came off a four-day shift at the fire station and normally he'd be asleep by now.

"No, nothing's wrong," he replies, smiling as he takes a mug down from the top shelf of the cabinet above the microwave. He's so tall, he doesn't even have to reach. "It's just that the sun is shining and I wanted to spend a day with my family. So I decided to pump my body with some caffeine and stay awake. Sorry I scared you."

With a sigh, I walk over to the pantry and pull out the morning's cereal selection. "That's okay, Daddy. But you really should get some sleep — we can all go to the park tomorrow."

He chugs back a giant gulp of steaming, black coffee and shakes his head.

"No way! Tomorrow it might rain. You have to take your chances while you've got them. Come on, Lora, it's Saturday. Let's go to the park. We could all use a little fresh air and I can sleep later. I've got a few days off coming to me."

Even though I know how badly he needs the sleep, I agree to the plans. As big a man as he is, my father exudes a quiet teddy-bear kind of charm. My whole life, I've never been able to resist him.

After we've all eaten breakfast, he picks up Mommy in his burly arms and places her gently into her wheelchair. My sisters and brother fly around the house with excitement when they hear the plans for the day. It's been an agonizingly long winter this year and they're dying to get outside and play. After we dig our spring coats out of the closet, we set off for the park.

Outside, the fresh air smells like mud pies and earthworms. I lead the way, holding the dogs' leashes in one hand and carrying a small bag filled with sand toys in the other. Daddy lets Allie help him push Mommy's wheelchair down the sidewalk, manoeuvering it carefully around the streams trickling from the last stubborn islands of melting snow. It doesn't take long for Chelsea and Cody to race ahead of the pack on their tricycles. They're energized by the warmth of the sun and excited to leave their hats and mittens at home and feel the breeze on their skin. The dogs bark at the small, spinning wheels of the trikes as they pass.

Mommy also looks like she's enjoying the outing. She sits with her face tilted toward the sky, like a sunflower following the light. Her eyes are closed and there's a little smile playing on her lips. I realize that this is one of the only times we've been anywhere together as a family this year.

When we arrive at the park, Chelsea and Cody dash straight to the swings and Daddy follows close behind to give under-dogs and rocket-ship rides. Freed from their leashes, the dogs chase each other around the grass, stopping only to sniff at the odd tree or rock. Allie starts digging a castle in the damp sand and I sit on the bench beside Mommy's wheelchair to keep her company.

From the toy bag, I pull out the pad of paper and pen I'd stashed before leaving home. There's a new homework assignment I'm hoping to work on today and I figure this is as good a time as any to get started.

"What are you doing, Lora?" I hear Mommy ask. Her words are clear and her voice is strong. Maybe it's the sun or maybe it's the fresh air, but whatever the reason, this is definitely sounding like a good day.

"We just finished a session on Shakespeare in my English class," I explain. "For our final assignment of the year, Miss Wall wants us to try writing some poetry of our own."

"Shakespeare, eh?" she replies. "Are you going to write your poem in iambic pentameter, too?"

I laugh and shake my head. "Miss Wall said not to worry too much about meter or rhyme at this point. Just get our thoughts and feelings out."

"Well, that sounds very interesting ... what will you write about?"

"Um ... I don't know yet," I say with a shrug. "I think I'll wait for something to inspire me."

Mommy nods and turns her head toward the swing set. Alone with my thoughts, I smooth out the paper, uncap my pen, and wait for the words to arrive. I'm excited about this assignment. I've never written a poem before, but because I've heard so much poetry lately, I figure there's a good chance that, like all things academic, it'll come naturally. The Sunday-night poetry readings at the coffee shop have been incredible. Madison's gone up to read a couple of her poems and has received some really good feedback. She's been urging me to read something, too. Maybe if I can work up the courage, I'll try it. I'd like to get my poem as perfect as possible before I hand it in to Miss Wall. A really good mark in English will keep my grade point average nice and high. All I have to do now is figure out what to write about.

"Poetry is all about feelings," Miss Wall had written on the blackboard after she'd given out the assignment. "A poem is pure emotion on paper. Choose a subject that moves you and start to write."

I watch the kids play and wait for something to move me. My thoughts travel back to the days when Mommy used to bring me to this same park. It's hard to believe that only a few years ago I was still young enough to forget my troubles in a playground. I look at the swings and remember the day when I was five years old and Mommy was trying so hard to teach me how to swing on my own. I couldn't understand the mechanics of it. When to push, when to pull, how to use my little body to propel that swing up into the sky. I remember getting frustrated very quickly and stomping away in a huff.

"I can't do it," I whined. "Why can't you just push me like you always do?" But Mommy wouldn't let me give up.

"Sit with me, Lora," she said, taking a seat on an empty swing and pulling me onto her lap. With her hands covering mine, we gripped the chains together. "Hold on tight now," she whispered into my hair as she leaned back and began to swing. "I won't let you fall."

And, although my body felt slippery on top of hers, I knew she wouldn't.

Up, down, push, pull — we moved slowly back and forth, as if to the lilt of a perfectly timed song. She under me, teaching me the rhythm with the sway of her own body. I sat on top of her, feeling her breath in my ear and her heart beating against my back as we swung higher and higher until our feet were kicking the sky in victory.

"Lora, are you okay?" I hear Mommy say. I turn my head toward her and for a moment I'm shocked at the sight of the frail woman beside me. Physically, she's aged three decades in the few short years since her diagnosis. Her body is so weak and tired and I sometimes marvel that it still performs the basic functions of living. How is it possible to have lost so much of my mother in such a short time?

She lifts a thin arm and reaches out to take my hand. My heart aches for those strong hands that gripped the chains over mine and for those healthy arms that once held me so tight as we raced through the air on that narrow rubber perch.

"I'm fine, Mommy," I reply, forcing my voice not to quiver. I smile and give her hand a light squeeze. We've switched places in these past three years. Now I'm the strong one.

A shadow creeps across the ground. I look up and see that a thick layer of grey clouds has overtaken the sky. Without the sun's heat, this early spring day quickly turns chilly. It doesn't take long for the little ones to start complaining about their cold fingers and ears. We pack up our buckets and shovels, balls, and trikes to go home. The words of my poem come to me as we walk. I dash upstairs to write them down as soon as we get there.

I can't sleep that night, so I creep out of my room, walk down the hall and slip into bed with my parents. Daddy is passed right out and snoring loudly. He's always so tired when he comes off a shift, only the sound of a siren would wake him up. Mommy's taken her nighttime meds and is deeply asleep, too. She doesn't move a muscle when I crawl into bed, lay my head down on her shoulder, and curl my body around her — just like she did to me all those years ago on the swing.

"I love you, Mommy," I whisper into her hair. She doesn't hear me, but it doesn't matter. Just being close to her is comforting enough. I snuggle into the reassuring warmth of her body and try not to let myself wonder how much more of my mother I have left to lose.

Today ...

tabby

"I hate them ... I hate them ... I hate them ... I hate them ..." moans the voice in the toilet stall beside me.

Holy crap! The girl on the other side is freaking out! She sounds like a total wreck. She's wailing so loudly that my ears are hurting.

I prop my elbows onto my knees, lean forward on the toilet seat and wonder what on earth to do about the sob-fest going on just inches to my left.

Should I say something to her? If so, what? I raise my hand to knock on the stall, but lower it a second later. Maybe I should respect her privacy and let her cry alone? I mean, this girl is clearly in the middle of some kind of breakdown. I know that *I* like to be left alone when I'm crying my guts out — it's something I've done a lot of over these past few weeks. But what if this girl is different? What if she wants someone to hear her?

I don't know the answer to that question. And before I have the chance to figure it out, my thoughts are thrown off by a loud, honking nose blow.

I look at my watch and see that there's still twelve

minutes left of the lunch period. *What should I do about this?* I bite my bottom lip and scratch my head in frustration.

This whole situation is awkward. All I wanted was a quiet place to hide out until lunch was over. I didn't ask to be thrown into the middle of a stranger's emotional breakdown. I'd like to walk away quietly and give this girl the privacy she needs. But that would mean leaving the bathroom and going back out *there* ... and facing *them.* That's something I just can't bring myself to do.

"I hate them ... I hate them ... I hate them ... I hate them ..." I hear the girl moan again. The voice sounds familiar, but I can't place it. I probably know her if she goes to this school. I lean a bit farther down and look at her shoes again. She's wearing a pair of plain, beat-up black sneakers — definitely not designer. Definitely not expensive. Maybe I don't know her, after all. I mean, nobody I know wears shoes like that!

The moaning begins to quiet down a little until all I can hear is a muffled weeping. I look at my watch again and sigh. Eight minutes left. God! This is torture! I can't sit here listening anymore. I raise my hand and, against all my better judgment, tap against the side of the stall with my knuckle.

"Um ... hello? You okay in there?" I whisper.

There's a pause and I hear the girl take a long, shuddery breath.

"No, I'm not," she replies with a shaky, brittle voice. "Not at all."

Her voice cracks open on the last word and I can hear the crying start up again. I stare at the green graffiti-scrawled wall and try to think of what to say.

"Um … do … do you need help?" I ask, not sure what else to do.

There's a small laugh. That must be a good sign, right? My heart rises a bit. Maybe she's feeling better. And then:

"I don't know … can you transfer me to another country?"

I laugh, too. Hey, anything to help lighten the mood a bit, right?

"Come on …" I coax, "… whatever happened, it can't be *that* bad!"

For some reason, I'm determined to help this girl feel better.

"Yes, it really is that bad," comes the reply. "My life feels so hopeless. My mother has an awful disease and my father is never home and I never have any time for myself. And I don't have any friends. And then those boys go and treat me like that? Grabbing me and pushing me on the ground? What did I ever do to deserve that? I just hate them all so much!"

Damn it! The voice is so low now it's barely more than a breath. I'm losing her! Who is this girl, anyway?

"Who?" I urge, hoping to keep her talking. "Who's 'them'?"

"Everyone!" she sobs. "This whole entire school! The things they say hurt so much. And those disgusting emails never stop. I mean, how can people be so cruel? I can't even get peace in my own home."

I think about the wall posts I got last night on Facebook and tears spring to my eyes. The words were so vicious.

Phoney!

Bitch!

Thief!

Die!

You suck!

Burn in Hell!

I take a deep breath and let it out slowly.

"Yeah ... I know what you mean," I say. "Maybe I can transfer to another country, too." I can't bring myself to laugh this time. In fact, as much as I try to keep them in, more tears are coming. They slide down my cheeks in salty streams. Remembering my promise to myself, I struggle to swallow my sobs. No matter how bad it gets, I don't want anyone to catch me crying. My nose starts to run. I reach for some toilet paper to wipe it. Damn it — I chose the loser stall with no supplies!

"Um ... could you pass me some paper please?" I whisper, trying to keep my voice from breaking. "I'm all out in here."

I hear the sound of rolling, then a short rip and then a thin, freckled hand appears under the stall with a wad of paper.

"Here," says the voice with a sniff.

"Thanks."

I wipe my nose and frown. Even her hand is familiar. Who is this girl? Should I ask? Does she know who *I* am?

"You don't sound too happy, either," says the voice softly. "Are *you* all right?

She sounds concerned. For a moment I actually consider telling her some of my problems. After all, it sounds like she could probably understand. I lean my head up against the stall and try to figure out which part I should start with. My messed-up parents? The incriminating email I leaked? Being the most hated kid in school?

But before I can do that, the first bell rings. I glance at my watch and see that it's time to go back to class. With a final wipe of my eyes, I undo the lock and swing the door open at the exact same time as my cry-buddy does. We turn to face each other and my stomach does a somersault. I can't help letting out a small scream of shock when I see who it is.

Oh.

My.

God!

Lora

Oh my God!

It's Tabby Freeman! I'd been opening up my heart and soul to the head piranha! I hear my own pulse pounding in my ears as we stand there, staring at each other in astonishment. Predator facing prey. I swallow a hard lump in my throat, close my eyes and steel myself for the inevitable verbal attack.

"Oh, um … hi," she says.

My eyes fly open.

That's it? Hi??

I'm so stunned, I can't even think of a reply. So I don't say anything at all.

"I didn't know it was you … um, *Lora*," she says.

My face burns when I hear her say my name. We've known each other since kindergarten and that was definitely a first. I can tell from the hesitation in her words that she had to stop herself from saying Frog-face.

"Well, um …" She shuffles her feet and looks wistfully at the door. It's clear she wants to go. My skin itches with her desperation.

"Are you going to be okay now?" she asks, looking back at me.

I shrug and stare down at my feet.

What do you care? I think. *Just go!*

Suddenly Tabby's hand is on my arm. The warmth of her touch slices through my shirt and burns the skin beneath. I look up and see her round cat's eyes staring deeply into my own.

"*Are* you?" she asks again. Her question is sincere.

I shake my head and answer as honestly as I can.

"I don't think so."

She takes a long breath.

"Listen, Lora, don't let the bastards grind you down. Stand up for yourself. If they see that you're a fighter, they won't be so hard on you."

My chin drops down and smacks into my neck. I don't know what's shocked me more ... having Tabby Freeman offer me advice or hearing her quote a line from a Margaret Atwood novel? The funny thing is that Madison's been telling me the same thing for months now. But somehow, having one of my tormentors say it makes the point all that more clear.

"So? Do you think you can you do that?" she asks.

I shrug my shoulders and change the subject.

"What about you?" I say. "Are *you* going to be okay?"

She drops my arm and takes a small step back. For the briefest of moments, her face opens up and I can see her vulnerability fly across her features. And then it's gone — like a tiny hole in a thick layer of cloud that flashes a glimpse of blue before sealing up the sky again.

"Of course," she says after a small pause. "I'll land on my feet ... I always do."

But she's too late to convince me. I've already seen the doubt in her eyes.

The words are still hanging in the air when the second bell goes off, ripping through the tiled bathroom with a piercing screech. This strange little confession-session is over.

As Tabby turns to leave, I can see the tear-soaked, wadded-up toilet paper still clutched in her hand. I watch her walk away and I wonder where she learned how to lie so well. But then I remember about her parents.

tabby

Sam is barking. Chasing rabbits in his dreams again.

"Go back to sleep, boy," I mumble, rolling over in my bed. It's late. Or maybe it's early ... the room is too black to tell. Sam barks again and suddenly I smell the smoke. I lift my head and open my eyes. Even through the darkness, I can make out the thin, grey haze that is filling the room. Panic grips my chest as my dreams fall away and reality closes in.

"Fire! Fire!" I shriek to no one in particular, bolting upright in bed. Desperately, I begin feeling around the covers for Sam. After a few seconds, I find him standing beside my bed, still whining and barking for me to get up. He hadn't been dreaming about rabbits after all — the smell of smoke must have woken him up. I pull him into my arms and kiss his floppy ears.

"Thank you, Sam, you smart dog! I'm awake now, it's okay. We've got to get out of here, boy!" I say. Holding him by the collar, I slide out of bed, stagger to my bedroom door and grab the knob. The metal is hot.

I yank the sleeve of my pajamas down over my hand like a mitt, turn the knob, and fling the door open.

Immediately a big, grey cloud of smoke flies at my face, stinging my eyes and filling my mouth with the taste of burning house.

Oh God! This is really bad! I think, squeezing my eyes shut to keep the smoke out. Dropping Sam's collar, I cover my mouth with my hands to keep myself from breathing the toxic air that's rushing into my bedroom. But it doesn't work. A moment later I'm doubled over in a violent coughing fit. Scared, Sam crouches down onto the floor and starts to whine and bark again. He might be old and lazy, but he's smart enough to know that something is terribly wrong. As I cough, I rack my panicked brain, trying to remember what I'd been taught to do in a fire.

Stop, drop, and roll ... is that right? No, that's if your clothes are on fire. But wait ... dropping sounds good. Doesn't smoke rise? I look down at Sam who is flattening himself out on the floor beside me and covering his nose with his paws. I fall down to my stomach next to him and try to breathe. My coughing eases up a bit. Yes, the air is definitely a bit better down here.

"Come on, boy, follow me," I yell at Sam. On our tummies, we start making our way down the smoke-filled hallway. I crawl in front while Sam creeps behind. All the while, my mind is pounding with questions.

How did this happen?
Why aren't the fire alarms going off?
Where are my parents?
Oh no ... where's Nanny?

The air is so thick with smoke that I can't see where I'm going. My eyes are burning and my lungs are screaming with every breath. Another coughing fit seizes my body and I curl up into a ball, gasping for air until it passes. I open my eyes and try to look through the haze, but I can't see anything. I keep crawling toward my parents' room, checking every couple of seconds to make sure Sam is still with me. My whole chest feels like it's burning up. I cough so much, I have to stop again. I try to catch my breath, but it's like fighting a losing battle. I struggle to get air into my lungs. I see the flames just as I reach the top of the stairs. They're climbing up the living room curtains, licking at the ceiling, swallowing Catherine's prize Biedermeier couches whole. Most of the main floor is on fire! How are we going to get out?

Shutting my eyes to block the smoke, I blindly grope my way in the direction of my parents' room. When I get to their door, I push it open and scream as loud as my smoke-filled lungs will allow:

"Mom? Dad? Are you here? The house is on fire!"

Before the answer comes, I collapse into another coughing fit. This one is so bad, it feels like it will never stop. Sam grabs my pajamas between his teeth and pulls, trying to keep me going. But I'm drowning from the smoke. Every breath is a struggle.

Giving up, Sam creeps over and licks my face. I reach up and stroke his ears. A cloud of little stars explodes in front of my eyes.

Suddenly, I hear someone else coughing beside me and feel a pair of strong hands lift my body up from under my arms. I peer through the smoke and the stars to see who it is, but before I can make out a face everything suddenly goes black.

Lora

Daddy is waiting in the car when I come out of the mall. I wave to him sheepishly through the windshield, hoping he's not upset. By the time we finished cleaning up the coffee shop after tonight's poetry reading, it was way past midnight.

"Hi, sorry I'm late," I say, jumping into the front.

"Aw, s'okay," he replies, leaning his large frame toward me for a kiss. Without a word of reproach, he turns the key and we wait while the engine coughs and chokes like a cat working out a hairball.

Our family car is a big, forest-green minivan with a dented front bumper. My parents bought it fifteen years ago when they found out they were expecting me. They always wanted a big family and their plan was to keep having kids until every seat in the car was filled. They almost got there, too … and then Mommy got sick.

Daddy says that our old car is tougher than any of the new cars on the market today. But it shakes and rattles like there's rocks under the hood and I know it's only a matter of time before it conks out on us for good.

Dear God, when that happens, I don't know what we'll do.

After a few more coughs, the engine turns over. I breathe a silent sigh of relief as Daddy puts it into gear and we pull away from the parking lot.

"So, did you get to read your poem tonight?"

"I did," I confess with a shy smile. It actually took me all night to work up the courage to do it. When I was done, the entire coffee shop rose to their feet and applauded. There were only about twenty people there but it was overwhelming and exhilarating and terrifying and amazing all at the same time. Maybe I'll be a poet instead. Or maybe I'll do both — a zoologist/poet.

"And I think they liked it," I add. "I guess it's ready to hand in now."

Daddy looks away from the road for a quick second and raises his eyebrows at me.

"So does that mean I'm going to get a chance to hear it one of these days?"

"Um ... maybe," I reply, twirling my hair around my finger. "But I don't know if it's your taste ... it's a bit sad."

Hoping the subject will end, I turn my face toward the window and stare out into the night. Why is it so much easier to bare your soul to strangers than to the people closest to you? It's late and the streets are almost deserted. Through the darkness, I can just make out the outline of a big, grey cloud of smoke rising up above the rooftops. There's no mistaking what it is. I jab my finger against the glass and yell:

"Look! There's a fire!"

Daddy ducks his head down to get a better view of the smoke and lets out his signature monotone whistle.

"You're right … and it's a big one."

Without even a second's hesitation, he turns the car in the direction of the rising cloud.

I turn to look at him in surprise.

"Are we going?"

"Of course we're going."

"But … but you don't have any of your equipment here," I start to protest. "And Mommy's waiting for us at home. Can't we just call the department and let them handle it?"

Daddy doesn't answer and his silence speaks for itself. I know every instinct in his body is compelling him to follow that dark cloud. He drives toward it, completely ignoring the speed limit. After all his years of firefighting, Daddy must have developed a sixth sense for smoke because it only takes him a few minutes to find the source.

When I get my first look at the blazing building, my heart plunges into my stomach. It's a huge house, three stories tall and set far back from the road across a massive, landscaped lawn. The entire front part of the building is engulfed in flames.

Daddy parks our car across the road from the house,

digs his cellphone out of his pocket and immediately calls 911.

"This is Lieutenant Froggett," he barks into the phone. "There's a fire at 45 Thurston Road and I need backup. Send every available engine now!"

Tossing the phone onto the dashboard, he throws open the door and unfolds his big body from the car with impressive speed. I lean across the seat and yell after him through the open door:

"Wait, Daddy! What are you doing?"

But of course, he doesn't listen.

"Stay there!" he commands over his shoulder as he runs up the grass toward the house. Before he reaches the front door, it bursts open and three pajama-clad people appear through a cloud of black smoke. A blonde woman and a dark-haired man carrying a girl in his arms all stagger away from the burning house, across the lawn to the safety of the street. A little beagle follows closely behind the family. As they get closer, I recognize the girl in the man's arms.

It's Tabby Freeman!

I watch in horror as the man lays her down on the grass right next to the sidewalk. Her eyes are closed, her body is limp, and it looks like she's unconscious. The blonde woman is screaming so loudly that I can hear her from the car.

"Darling, wake up! Please! Somebody help! Help my daughter!"

Daddy reaches them and I can see him loosen her clothing and begin AR. Ignoring Daddy's instructions, I jump out of the car and run toward them. My knees are shaking so hard, I worry they'll give out. But, as terrified as I am, I have to go.

As I approach I can see that the blonde woman is sobbing and clutching onto the man, whose face is scraped and bleeding down his neck. Even though they're both sooty-skinned and dishevelled, I recognize David and Catherine Freeman from their pictures in the newspaper. They look very different — he's grown a beard since the scandal broke and she looks much younger without all the glossy makeup.

I stand behind Daddy and hold back tears as he tries to revive Tabby on the front lawn. After a minute, she lifts her head slightly and looks around. Even in the darkness, I can see how red and irritated her eyes are. She looks terrible. Her nose is rimmed with black soot and she's so pale, she's practically glowing in the dark.

"Darling!" Mrs. Freeman cries, leaning down to hug her. Her pink, lacy nightie hangs open revealing a shocking amount of cleavage. Under normal circumstances, I might have been embarrassed for her. But with the fire raging behind us, I don't give it much thought. "Are you okay?" she shrieks, clutching Tabby's hand to her heart. "Oh, sweetheart! I was so scared!"

Daddy takes Mrs. Freeman's arm and gently tries to pull her back.

"Please give this girl room — she needs air."

But she shakes her head, refusing to let go of her daughter's hand. With a sigh of resignation, he picks up Tabby's other hand and starts to measure the pulse in her wrist.

"You're going to be okay. I'm a firefighter and I'm here to help." His voice is calm and his words soothing and slow. He looks up momentarily from Tabby and directs a question to her parents: "Is there anyone else still inside this house?"

Mr. and Mrs. Freeman look at each other and frown, like they're trying to figure out a math equation. Hearing the question, Tabby's eyes dart from face to face, trying to remember the answer. Suddenly, a look of horror flashes across her features and she struggles to sit up.

"Nanny Beth!" she cries, clutching an ashen hand onto Daddy's sleeve. "Oh my God! She's still inside!"

I barely recognize her voice. She's short of breath and her throat is so hoarse from smoke inhalation that her words crackle like dry leaves.

Daddy takes Tabby by the shoulders and gently guides her back down onto the grass. "Please lie still … you need to rest. Just tell me where she is. Which part of the house?"

"Her room is in the basement!" Tabby moans, resisting his help and pushing herself back up. "Please! She must still be down there. You can get there through the garden window at the back of the house. Oh God! Please go get her!"

He looks up at the burning house and shakes his head firmly.

"I'm sorry, but I don't have my equipment with me. It's just too dangerous. We'll have to wait for the fire engines to arrive. They'll be here soon and I'll let them know where to look. Now please stay calm."

Daddy turns to speak privately with Mrs. Freeman.

"Your daughter's pulse is a bit weak. I think she's in shock. She needs to lie down and stay warm. I need you to encourage her to do that."

She nods vigorously, still clutching onto Tabby's hand. Then he points to Mr. Freeman and commands:

"Go get a blanket from a neighbour and some clean water for her eyes. And call 911 again and tell them to get those engines here now!"

It's strange to watch my father giving orders to Mr. Freeman — a man who not long ago was one of the most powerful businessmen in the whole province. I half expect Mr. Freeman to refuse. Instead, he nods and runs off into the darkness toward the street. As I watch him go, I can see bright orange flames from the inferno reflecting in the windows of our car. I look back toward the smoldering house. We're about twenty metres away but I can feel the heat from the fire on my face. It's scorching my skin like a bad sunburn.

Mrs. Freeman tries to calm her daughter, but Tabby refuses to lie quietly. "No! Nanny's trapped in there!" she sobs. "She'll die if we leave her! I'll go get her myself if I have to!"

She struggles to get to her feet and it takes both my

father and her mother to hold her back. She claws at them like a tethered wildcat, trying to get loose. Just as Mr. Freeman arrives back with the blanket and water bottles, the sound of broken glass shatters the night. I look back at the burning house and see that the heat from the fire is smashing the windows. One by one they burst — like there's a kid shooting them down with a slingshot. Flames are shooting out from every opening. I cover my face and turn toward Tabby, who's staring at the house in horror. That's the moment when her sobs turn into screams.

"Please! It's getting worse! You could just break one of the basement windows and let her out. Please don't leave her in there! She'll die if you do!"

I can't imagine anybody going back into that building. But I know Daddy too well. I can tell by the look in his eyes that he's going to do it. He looks at me, his face silently asking permission to go in. I want to stop him, but I know I can't. Daddy was born to save lives. He would never leave a person in need.

"I'll be okay, I promise," he says, locking his eyes with mine. "You know me … I won't do anything stupid."

"Daddy, please … " I start to say. But he doesn't even wait for me to finish. Before I know it, he wets his sleeve with some of the water, clasps it over his face and dashes toward the burning building.

I stand there in shock. A terrible thought creeps into my head, but I push it away. It creeps back again and again, stronger and louder each time. I keep pushing it away until

I can't ignore it anymore and it screams through my brain like a siren.

Oh God! What if he doesn't make it back out? What if he dies in there? What'll we do without Daddy?

I close my eyes and shake the awful thought from my head. As agonizing as it is, there's nothing left for me to do but wait. With my eyes closed, my other senses are heightened. The air smells like burned wood. The house is crackling and popping like a campfire. My nose and throat scream for fresh air. I open my eyes again and see thick, black smoke billowing up into the sky. A giant mushroom cloud above our heads.

I look at Tabby and wonder what she's feeling. I can't imagine what it's like to watch your house and everything you own go down in flames right in front of your eyes. But it seems like the only thing she's worried about is the woman trapped in the basement. Slumped on the ground, she sobs and calls for her nanny over and over in a low, haunting moan. Mrs. Freeman sits on the ground beside her and wraps Tabby in her arms to soothe her. Despite Daddy's instructions to give her room to breathe, she's hugging her daughter so tight it looks like she'll never let go. Tears spring to my eyes as I watch them. More than ever before, I want my mother strong and healthy and here to comfort me, too.

Some neighbours gather to watch the blaze and offer their help. Someone hands me a jacket and I accept, grateful for a stranger's kindness (although with the heat from the fire, the night air doesn't feel as cold as I know it should be). Agonizing seconds tick by.

I hear a whining at my feet and look down to see the dark little beagle cowering on the grass. I kneel down to pet him and his little body quivers with fright under my hands. Leaning my face close to his, I rub the length of his nose and murmur soothing words into his floppy black ears. After a few minutes, I'm able to calm him down. Surprisingly, I feel a bit calmer, too. Helping this little dog is keeping my mind away from what's going on inside the burning house. Seconds later, the beagle stops whining and starts to lick my face. I stroke his shiny fur, happy to have something to hold on to. That's when Tabby finally notices me.

"Lora?" she gulps through her tears. "W-what are you doing here?"

"I was coming home from work when I saw the smoke," I say, still hugging the little dog. "That's my father in there trying to save your nanny."

My voice breaks on the last few words. Tabby doesn't reply. She just looks at me and in that instant, an understanding passes between us. Time pauses, the flames retreat, and for that moment she sees into my heart and I see into hers. I realize that we're experiencing this moment with the same eyes. Both of us waiting, needing, praying for the person we love most to come out of that fire.

Suddenly, Mrs. Freeman screams, breaking our connection.

"They're coming out! Look!"

With the wail of fire engines emerging from the distance, I look up and see Daddy walking across the lawn, carrying a small woman in his arms. She's as limp as a rag doll and her face is black from the smoke, but her eyes are open and she's definitely alive. And so is my father.

Releasing the dog, I fall to my knees on the soft grass as my body heaves with relief. One small word pulses through my head, as if to the beat of my own pounding heart.

Daddy ... Daddy ... Daddy ...

tabby

It's the last day of school. With a loud clank, I lift the stiff handle of my locker, pull open the door, and start to clear everything out. Piece by piece, I shove my stuff into my open backpack. Books, binders, gym shoes, makeup, magazines, pictures. This junk in my locker is pretty much the only stuff I have left in the world ... the only things that will be coming with me to my new home.

Our giant, custom-built house on Thurston Road has been burned to a crisp. Although the firefighters worked for hours to save it, all that was left at the end of that awful night was a big, museum-sized pile of ashes. Along with the house, we also lost all our possessions — our furniture, clothing, jewellery, photos. The Bentley and the BMW had both burned in the garage. And even David's flashy Rolex couldn't survive the flames. The fire investigators found a scorched, twisted lump of gold where his nightstand once stood. There's nothing of our old life left. And I don't feel the slightest bit depressed about it.

I've known for a while now that those things didn't belong to us, anyway.

My backpack fills up pretty fast. I squat down and try to zip it shut, but it's too full to close completely. As I struggle with the zipper, a parade of shoes zoom past me, barely touching the floor in their rush for freedom. Last year I was one of them. Excited for summer and gushing about parties and plans. This year, they just ignore me and I return the favour. It's easier for everyone that way. Giving up on the zipper, I stand and hoist the backpack onto my shoulders, careful not to spill anything. With a final slam of the locker, I'm gone.

I won't miss this place when we move. I'm actually happy for the chance to start all over again. I mean, how many people get an opportunity like this? A fresh start in a place where nobody knows my family ... nobody loves us or hates us for what we own or what we've done. A place where kids will like me for who I am. Or maybe they won't even like me at all. Either way, at least nobody will pretend anymore. For the first time, I'm going to have real parents, real friends ... and a real me.

I can't wait.

There's just one last stop to make before I can leave this school behind. About a hundred more steps until I'm out of here forever and my new life can begin. I look down at my shoes and start counting my steps as I make my way through the busy hallway. All I have to do now is figure out how the hell I'm going to say *sorry*, *thank you*, and *goodbye* at the same time.

The countdown begins.

Ninety-nine … ninety-eight … ninety-seven …

The crowd still parts for me like it used to — but now it's more out of awkwardness than anything else. Nobody in this place knows what to say to me anymore. I'm the sour note in their fun celebration song. As I pass my classmates, I hear little bits and pieces of their conversations — lighthearted giggles, whispers of summer plans, and heartfelt promises to "keep in touch." The hall is practically pulsing with joy.

Seventy-six … seventy-five …

Lined, loose-leaf papers carpet the way. The floors are littered with trashed tests, essays, assignments. Words tossed aside like garbage, never to be thought of again. Kind of like me.

Fifty-one … fifty … forty-nine …

As I get closer to my last stop, I start thinking about yesterday's conversation with Catherine. She'd knocked on my door late last night, just as I was trying to get comfortable on the foamy, floppy hotel pillow. A two-room suite at the Bayview Hotel — that's where we'd been staying since the fire.

"Hi … mind if I come in?" she asked softly from the doorway.

"Sure. What's up?" I replied, rising up on my elbows.

Letting herself into the room, she let the heavy door close with a click behind her. She hovered there in the entryway. I could see the fire exit instructions hanging right behind her head — the first thing I did after we checked in was memorize them.

I motioned for my mother to come closer. She was dressed in a simple, white hotel robe and slippers and her hair was pulled back into a long ponytail. We were all making do on the bare minimum of stuff these days, which must have been especially hard on a clothes horse like Catherine. This whole experience has been pretty humbling for her.

"Well, I just wanted to let you know that it's done," she said, taking a seat at the foot of the bed. At first I didn't know what she was talking about. She must have seen the confusion in my eyes.

"You know ... the liquidation," she explained. "Your father and I finished selling off the last of our assets today. It's all done."

Of course, then I understood. Last week, my parents and their lawyers had been able to arrange a plea bargain. If David and Catherine paid back everything they stole with interest, they would avoid criminal charges. They were given ten days to liquidate all their assets and sell everything that wasn't ruined in the fire.

Liquidate.

Funny word, huh? Before all this happened, I thought it meant what Dorothy did to the Wicked Witch of the West.

"So you sold all of it?"

Catherine closed her eyes and took a deep, long breath.

"All of it. The stocks, bonds, investments, chequing accounts, savings accounts, the vacation home in Florida — and even the land where our house used to be."

She pulled her robe tightly around her as she spoke, like she was suffering from a sudden chill. Without even thinking, I pulled the blanket back and patted the mattress, inviting her to join me. Poor Sam yipped with irritation as she crawled in. He wasn't used to sharing my bed with anyone else. Catherine put her head next to mine on the floppy pillow. Up close, I could see her natural brown roots pushing through her scalp. In all the years she's been dying it blonde, she'd never once let the roots show before. Except for the odd gray strand, it was the exact same colour as mine.

She must have noticed me looking at her roots because she put a hand up to cover her hairline and smiled.

"I've been thinking about going back to my natural brown. I think I'm ready for some changes."

I knew she was telling the truth. In fact, she'd already changed a lot since the fire. I think we all have. When the investigators told us that the batteries in the smoke alarm were way past their expiration date, I was horrified. I was so worried that Catherine would freak on Nanny Beth and blame her for everything we lost. But, surprisingly, she didn't. Maybe it's because Nanny was getting ready to move back to the Philippines. She told us that her whole near-death experience in the fire had made her rethink her life. She was desperate to be with her daughter again. I was devastated when she told me she was going, but not completely surprised. Like I said before, I kind of always knew she'd leave me one day. And maybe this timing was right after all. Pretty soon, my parents and I will be moving to an apartment that'll be way too small for a nanny. And this was our shot at being a real family for the first time.

Okay, I have to admit that there was a small part of me that worried I was taking a risk by trusting them. After all, David and Catherine have been letting me down since the day I was born. But my heart was telling me to go for it. After losing everything else in my life, it was a chance I was willing to take.

"So, I have a little present for you," Catherine said, reaching into the pocket of her robe. When she pulled her hand back out, it was clenched into a loose fist.

"It's time to give you this."

When she opened her hand, my heart rose in my chest.

"Grandma's bracelet?" I gasped, sitting up. "Why do you still have it? I mean, didn't the police make you sell everything?"

She smiled and reached for my wrist.

"Yes, they made us sell everything that was ours. But remember — this bracelet was in *your* name. Grandma specifically left it to you, so they couldn't take it. I figure it's time for you to have it. I'm just sorry I didn't give it to you sooner."

She slipped it around my wrist and fastened the clasp. I stared down at my arm, not knowing what to say. I'd waited so long to see this bracelet again — and here it was. Immediately, I raised it up to my nose and took a deep breath. I had been hoping it would still smell like Grandma's favourite rose perfume — the one she used to dab on her wrists every day. But after three sniffs, I lowered my wrist in disappointment. The bracelet didn't smell like anything at all — any lingering trace of perfume had vanished along with Grandma. My head suddenly filled with memories of her — her house, her stories, her sparkly blue eyes. I tried to imagine her wedding day when Grandpa fastened this very bracelet onto her wrist as a symbol of his love. She was only eighteen then — not much older than I was now. And then I started to cry.

Twenty-four ... twenty-three ...

I'm almost there. I hike my bursting backpack up a little higher as I make my way down the hall for the last time. Grandma's bracelet clanks against my wrist with every step. It feels funny there — heavy and kind of awkward. Not at all like I remembered it from those times she used to let me try it on. It's strange — I thought wearing her bracelet again would be a reminder of my grandmother and how much she loved me. But it's not. Instead, it feels like a chain pulling me back to the awful days when Catherine was trying to get rid of me. And I didn't want to remember those days anymore. I wanted to put them behind me and start looking toward the future.

I glance up from my shoes and see faces turning away as I approach, but I don't really care. They're strangers, every one of them. No one here ever really knew me. There's really only one person in this school that I need to say goodbye to. Although I've never visited her locker before, I know exactly where it is. Actually, it was pretty impossible not to know considering how many times it had been graffitied and vandalized over the past few years. Just a few more steps to go.

Nine ... eight ... seven ...

Lora

My feet bounce a bit as I jostle my way through the jubilant crowd toward my locker. School's over and the hallways reek with the sweaty excitement of newly liberated teenagers. I almost feel like celebrating along with everyone else. For the first time in my life I'm actually looking forward to my summer. And I don't even mind the idea of coming back here next year. Life has changed for me since the fire at the Freeman's house. Believe it or not, I'm not Frog-face anymore. Well ... at least not most of the time, anyway. There are still a few stubborn piranhas and pit bulls who refuse to give it up. Probably more out of habit than anything else.

Maybe they're being nicer to me because they've lost their leader. Without Tabby to look up to, they seem confused — like honeybees after the queen has died. They don't attack in packs and most of them seem to have lost their predatory spirit. Or maybe it's because I took Tabby Freeman's advice and started standing up for myself. Or maybe there's another reason … maybe they're being nicer to me because I'm related to a bona fide hero.

A week after the Freeman fire, Daddy was awarded a bravery medal by the mayor of our town in a special televised ceremony. Our whole family was there to watch him receive it — Mommy even put on makeup and her best dress for the occasion. She looked almost like her old self again, except of course for the wheelchair. The next day, Daddy's picture made it into all the newspapers and ever since, people have been stopping him on the street to ask for his autograph, or a picture, or just wanting to shake his hand. Daddy's sort of embarrassed by all the attention, but the rest of our family is bursting with pride. Mayor or no mayor — we always thought of him as a hero, anyway.

Sidestepping a renegade skateboarder, I turn the corner into the main hall and almost knock right into Tabby Freeman, who's standing near my locker. I blurt out a quick apology.

"Gosh, I'm sorry! I didn't see you there."

"That's okay," she says, holding up her hands. "I was actually waiting for you."

I can't hide my shock.

"*You* were waiting for *me*?" In all my years at this school, nobody's ever waited for me at my locker. I can see Tabby shifting her weight from one foot to the other. Is it possible that she's as nervous about talking to me as I am to her?

"You probably know that I'm not coming back here next year … so I just, um, wanted to say goodbye. And, well …

I'm sorry for being such a bitch all these years. I never really got the chance to know you and now I wish I had, Lora."

She says my name so naturally now. There's not even a hint of my old nickname hiding behind her words. I guess that's because she's not really a piranha anymore. I don't know what to say, so I shrug and say nothing.

"I also wanted to ask, well … how's your mom doing?" she continues, lowering her voice to a whisper — the way people do when they talk about something terrible.

I'm shocked at the question. How on earth does she know about Mommy? But then I remember back to that moment in the girl's bathroom when I'd sobbed out all my problems. I can feel my face beginning to warm up at the memory of that day. I know my skin is probably turning as red as my hair.

"She's about the same," I reply, bringing my hands up to cover my cheeks. "Thanks for asking."

Tabby leans her shoulder against the locker beside mine and lets her overstuffed backpack fall to her feet, like she's planning on hanging out for a while.

"And I wanted to tell you that I really liked the poem you wrote for English. It was … um … powerful."

This time, I blush so hard my face hurts. Last week, Miss Wall had asked us all to read our poems aloud in class. Most of the kids wrote pretty standard *roses are red, violets are blue* kind of stuff. So when my turn came, I was nervous. I didn't know if anyone would like it. When I was done reading, the kids stared at me in silence — completely the opposite reaction to what I'd received at the coffee shop poetry reading. I was a bit disappointed that nobody seemed to get it. But apparently, Miss Wall did. She gave me an A+ and asked me to come back after school to talk. At first, I thought she just wanted to have a friendly chat like we always do. But as soon as we were alone in the room, her pleasant face turned serious and the deep creases between her eyebrows came back.

"Lora, I'd like to help," she said.

I tried to play dumb, like the last time. "I don't know what you're talking about," I replied. But it didn't take her long to wrestle the truth out of me.

"Lora, your poem was very moving. But you couldn't have written it unless you were in a very dark place. I know you're having troubles."

She reached out and took my hand in hers. Her grip was warm, strong, and healthy. Suddenly, I felt tired. Really tired. After all this time, I didn't have the energy to put on the act anymore. Before I knew it, I was telling her everything.

Her face twitched with sadness while she listened to me speak. I really thought she might cry. When I was done, she said: "Lora, there are all kinds of places that can offer you and your family support — you just have to be willing to ask. I, for one, would be honoured if you would let me help."

Then she told me there was a summer camp for gifted children that she wanted to recommend me for. "I know someone on the board of directors, so I know exactly what kind of kid they're looking for. If I send them this poem along with a copy of your transcripts as evidence of your high academic ability, you're sure to get in for a two-week session. And they will probably be able to offer you full financial assistance as well."

I couldn't believe what I was hearing.

"I can't go away to camp! What about my family? I can't leave my mother alone with the kids."

But Miss Wall wouldn't take no for an answer.

"I'll speak to your father. Now that he's a friend of the mayor's, I'm sure he can arrange to get a few days off work. I'm certain that there are other firefighters' families who can lend a hand, too. And even I can help out. Teachers get the summer off, remember?"

I literally had to reach down and pinch my leg to make sure I wasn't dreaming. "You'd want to spend part of your vacation watching over a house full of little kids and animals?"

She laughed at that. "I have no other plans, my dear. And you could use a break."

It was like a miracle. I walked away from that class feeling like a helium balloon cut loose from its string. That was a week ago, and I still haven't completely floated back down to earth.

A group of kids race by Tabby and me, kicking up a flurry of paper as they run. The halls are rapidly emptying around us. Pretty soon, we'll be the only ones left in the building. I glance at my watch. If I don't leave soon, I'll be late to pick up Cody and Chelsea from their daycare. But Tabby doesn't look like she's going anywhere yet. Was she waiting for me to return the compliment about *her* poem?

"Um…I liked yours, too. Except, I'm not sure I really understood it."

"That's okay … it was actually about my grandmother and her experience during World War II."

She clears her throat and reaches for my arm. "Listen, before I go, I really want to thank you again for what you did that night of the fire. Nanny Beth … well, she means the world to me. I'll never forget how you and your father saved her life. *Never.*"

I think back to that moment on her lawn with the fire blazing in front of us — that moment when it seemed like she understood me better than anyone else in the world. "Yeah, I won't, either," I reply.

After that, there's an awkward pause. I shuffle my feet on the dusty floor, waiting for her to end the conversation and leave. But to my amazement, she starts speaking again. *Dear God, what's going on? Nobody at this school has ever been so interested in talking to me before.*

"So, you know I'm moving away next week … right?"

"Um … yes, I heard. Where are you going again?"

"The west coast. I'm pretty psyched at the idea of starting fresh — you know, in a place where people won't want to burn our house down. Hopefully nobody over there will have heard about my parents."

"Yeah … my dad told me that the fire was arson. I'm so sorry. I … I can't believe someone would do that to you. Do they have any idea who it was?"

Tabby shakes her head. "No. They're still investigating,

but at this point there aren't too many leads. The police said that there are probably hundreds of people in this town who hated us enough to set our house on fire. But now my father is beginning to think that the trail has gone cold."

I nod sympathetically. I know exactly how it feels to be hated like that.

"Well, I guess I better get going," she says, hiking her bulging backpack up onto her shoulders. That's when I notice the bracelet on her wrist.

"Wow! Is that yours?" I ask. Even though I knew it was rude to stare, the bracelet is so beautiful, I can't help myself.

She raises her arm stiffly and holds her wrist out for me to see.

"Thanks, it is now. But it used to be my grandmother's. She left it to me when she died."

I lean closer for a better view. It looks so delicate, I'm almost afraid to touch it.

"It must be an antique, then?"

Tabby nods and slowly twists the bracelet around her wrist with her other hand. "It's one of the only things my grandma took with her when she and my grandpa were hiding from the Nazis. They had to live in a dark cellar for five years and she said it gave her hope … she told me it …"

Tabby's voice trails off as a strange look comes over her face. Like her thoughts have temporarily flown off to another world.

"Tabby? Are you okay?"

Before I know what's happening, she's sliding the bracelet off her wrist and holding it out to me. Her eyes look wet.

"Here, Lora ... I'd like you to have it."

"W-what?" I sputter, taking a small step back. *Is she crazy?* "I ... I can't take your bracelet!"

She shakes it at me.

"Yes, you can. For a long time, I thought I needed it ... but I really don't. I'm ready for a fresh start. You and your father saved my life and Nanny Beth's. It's the least I can do to say thank you."

"No ... I'm sorry, but I can't accept it," I say, shaking my head.

Tabby takes a deep breath and reaches for my hand. When she speaks again her voice is so quiet, I can barely hear it over the sound of my pounding heart.

"Lora, I've stood back and watched you get bullied our whole lives. I probably could have stopped it ... but I didn't. My grandma lived in the shadow of the biggest bully that ever lived. This bracelet got her through it." She presses the string of pearls into my hand and forces my fingers closed around it.

"I *know* she'd want me to give it to you. There's not even a trace of doubt in my mind. Please, Lora — it's yours now. I hope things start to go better for you."

And with that, she gives me a quick hug and walks away.

I look down at the bracelet in my hands. Is it real? The pearls are deep and shiny and the little diamonds on the clasp sparkle under the fluorescent lights of the school hall.

My heart rises in my throat. I can barely draw a breath. How old is it if it had been hidden from the Nazis?

I hold the bracelet up to my face and peer at it until I can see the rounded reflection of my freckles and red hair in the shining surface of the pearls.

Tears sting my eyes.

Oh God!

It's the most beautiful thing I've ever seen in my life.

Rose
by Tabby Freeman

you started out pink but then
turned blue
when the big, black spider came
crawling for you

but he brought white light with his
saffron songs
to the grey underground where no
person belongs

in time, blue bruised to purple and
then back to pink
but was Rose ever restored?

what do you think?

Shadows
A poem by Lora Froggett

Shadows, shadows, darkened cloud,
Falling over like a shroud,
running through my dreams at night,
casting, creeping, spreading fright.
When the storm has come and gone,
the clouds persist straight through the dawn,
relentlessly they're pushing me,
blindly to my destiny.

Shadows, shadows all around,
pursuing me without a sound,
tracing steps and haunting f light,
heavy, stealing life's delight,
… growing each and every day,
everywhere and every way.
Should I resist and stand to fight,
I'll rise from shadows to the light.
Then the darkness will recede,
and my spirit will be freed.

Acknowledgements

This book wouldn't exist without the generous help of some very wonderful people. I would like to thank: Jordan Kerbel for propping me up, holding my hand, and always making me laugh; Jonah and Dahlia Kerbel for putting up with a few too many rushed dinners so I could squeeze in a bit of writing time; Shirley Pape, for inspiring me so profoundly with her strength and determination; Gordon Pape for his unconditional support of my writing (even when he doesn't particularly like what I'm writing about); Shirley Garfinkle for bravely volunteering to read the really rough drafts; Kim Pape-Green for her enthusiasm and exhausting nitpickiness; Kendra Pape-Green, for helping me nail down plot details; Sharon Arluck for her poetic finesse; Marina Cohen, for being a wonderful writing buddy (and offering me the use of her "forward instead of reply" anecdote); Dr. Francine Gerstein, my dear friend and medical fact-checker; Shelley Saunders-Greer, for giving this manuscript such a thorough once-over; Marsha Skrypuch and her Summer Writing Workshop; my tireless agent Margaret Hart for going through all the deets with her fine-tooth comb; Compuserve's Kidcrit literary forum for their eagle-eyed appraisals; and the Ontario Arts Council for supporting "starving artists" like myself through the Writers' Reserve Program.

Last but not least, I'd like to thank the incredibly hard-working team at Dundurn Press for believing in my words and transforming my stories into beautiful books.

Also by Deborah Kerbel

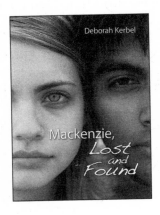

Mackenzie, Lost and Found

978-155002-852-2

$12.99

Nothing prepares fifteen-year-old Mackenzie Hill for the bombshell announcement that her and her dad, alone since the death of her mother a year ago, are moving to Jerusalem. The adjustment from life in Canada to life in Israel is dramatic, though it's eased somewhat by a new friend at school. But the biggest shock of all comes when Mackenzie faces the wrath of her new friends, new community, and even her own father after she begins dating a Muslim boy.

Snakes & Ladders
by Shaun Smith
978-1-55002-840-9 / $12.99

For as long as thirteen-year-old Paige Morrow can remember, the tree fort in the giant oak near her cottage in Ontario's Muskoka has been her sanctuary. Now everything is changing. She becomes concerned when the farmer who owns the property hires a creepy arborist. When Paige befriends the arborist's troubled teenage daughter and her group of rowdy locals, she is pulled into a maze of dark secrets and shocking truths that leads to a life-and-death confrontation.

Ghost Ride

by Marina Cohen

978-1-55488-438-4 / $12.99

Sam McLean is less than thrilled with the prospect of moving to the northern fringe of a small town called Ringwood. A nobody at his old school, fourteen-year-old Sam is desperate to be accepted by the cool kids and latches on to Cody Barns, aka Maniac. When Sam reluctantly joins Cody and his sidekick on their midnight ghost riding, a practice in which the driver and passenger climb onto the hood of their moving car and dance, something goes terribly wrong. As Sam struggles with his conscience, a haunting question remains: Who else knows the truth?

Available at your favourite bookseller.

www.dundurn.com